Forever ❧ Romances

Love's Design

Elee Landress

Forever 🌹 *Romances*

is an imprint of
Guideposts Associates, Inc.
Carmel, NY 10512

This Guideposts edition is published by
special arrangement with Thomas Nelson Publishers.

Printed in the United States of America.

To Susan and Mike
for a very special occasion

Chapter One

The morning was a blur of gray stone buildings, traffic-littered pavements, and a cacophony of horns sounding like an orchestra tuning their instruments before the performance.

As the cab raced through New York's garment district, a young woman stared from the window, her dark eyes animatedly alert as though she were the conductor of the symphonic sight and sound, relishing the rhythm and hum of another day getting underway.

This was no ordinary day for Bergitta Blakely. It was the apex of all she had striven for these past five years on the design staff of Worthington Clothiers, Ltd. Today she would take the step up that final rung of the ladder of success!

The cab swerved around the last corner, and she automatically took a compact from her purse. She was surprised by the glowing-eyed woman who looked back at her from the mirror. She had not been this excited since she was ten, and she told herself sternly to put her sophisticated mask in place. No one had patience with a designer who had gone goggle-eyed over her own success. She patted powder over the firm-toned skin, which fit smoothly over a delicate bone structure.

Except for the hair pulled too severely into a braided

knot at the back of her head and the horn-rimmed glasses she insisted on wearing for their studious effect, she might well have been one of the striking models who wore her designs with aplomb and poise. She denied this fact when it was brought up, almost resenting the classic features that molded her natural beauty. How could she ever be taken seriously as a designer as long as the professionals in the business kept insisting that modeling should have been her career?

But she had finally overcome it—and a lot of other obstacles as well! She snapped the compact closed with a smile of satisfaction and rummaged in her purse for cab fare.

The driver glanced over his shoulder. "Today's the day, aye?" She nodded, her beautifully shaped lips spreading into a happy smile that lit up the drab interior of the cab.

"This is it, Wally! Say one for me, okay?"

Grunting "Good luck" to the slim, lithe creature, he took the fare she offered. She sprang from the cab, barely missing the puddle of snowy slush that had not yet succumbed to the February thaw.

On the way up in the elevator she mentally rehearsed the order of the day. Clare L'aimant would arrive in half an hour for final fittings into her wedding gown, the *pièce de résistance* Bergitta had designed for the Worthington spring showing. The famous model would wear it when she exchanged vows with Jordan Wright Worthington III, heir to the Worthington fortune. Bergitta smiled. She couldn't believe her own good fortune. With the internationally famous model the center of the show, no expense had been spared in the ad campaign and preliminary publicity. Clare had insisted on it. She had also insisted on keeping her identity a secret until today at the ten o'clock press conference.

"That's fine with me, Clare," Bergitta grinned as she muttered to herself. "The more effective the timing, the better for my career." In three days every major department store and *haute couture* specialty shop would send their buyers to the most-talked-about show of the season. Not only would they be treated to the most brilliant fashions ever produced in the design world, the trousseau of Clare L'aimant, but they also would witness the wedding of the decade, second only to the marriage of Princess Di and Prince Charles.

She stepped onto the lush pile carpet of the mauve and chrome reception area and nodded good morning to Mindy.

"Bernie has an important message for you," the receptionist said anxiously. "She says not to do anything before you check in with her."

Bergitta tilted her head and rolled her eyes. Everyone tended to get hyper before a big show. "Tell her I'll be there shortly, Mindy. I want to say hello to Clare and make sure there aren't any problems with the fitting."

Even as she spoke, her administrative assistant appeared, white-faced. "B. G., this can't wait. Jordan wants to see you in his father's office immediately."

Seeing the interested look that leaped into Mindy's eyes, Bergitta held back a quick retort and walked past her assistant's office into her own inner sanctum.

"What is it, Bernie?" she asked calmly, waiting for an explanation from the frantically agitated woman. "What is so urgent that the happy bridegroom can't wait to see me?" The edge of sarcasm in her voice reflected the long-standing contempt she held for Jordan Wright Worthington, the parasite playboy. He thumbed his nose at the family business, making contributions only on the liability side of the ledger via his monthly paychecks for flying in to an occasional board meeting.

"Do you want it verbatim?" Bernie asked, then proceeded to deliver the sharply worded message.

B. G. turned on her heel and lifted the gray cashmere cape from her shoulders, revealing the matching fitted suit, accented with white bib and black bow tie. Black shoes and purse completed the smart executive look.

Flashes of sunlight shot highlights of deep umber through her dark hair as she strode across the floor to hang her cape on the coat rack. She calmly walked back to her desk and began to issue orders for the day as she unpacked her slimline leather briefcase.

Bernie's jaw dropped. "Aren't you going to J.W.'s office to see what Jordan wants?"

"I don't take my orders from Jordan. If J.W. wants to see me before the staff meeting at eleven, he will let me know."

Bernie began to twist the Kleenex in her hand. "I know you don't care much for Jordan, B. G., but this really sounded serious. I don't think you ought to ignore—" She was interrupted by the intercom.

"Bernie, has Ms. Blakely arrived yet?" a steel-edged voice inquired. There was static in the silence.

"Yes sir, she has."

A voice boomed back like the sudden descent of an electrical storm. "Then tell her I said to get in here and be quick about it!"

Bernie lifted one eyebrow as if to say, "See? I warned you."

B. G. was rising from her chair when Jordan hurtled through a side door which connected the two offices in the executive suite. He was beside her in a moment, seizing her under the elbow and propelling her to his father's office while the rotund Bernie looked on in astonishment.

Once in the short connecting hallway, with the door closed behind them, B. G. pulled away from the dark-haired, deep-complexioned man whose powerful agility and swift motions reminded her of a jungle cat.

"Suppose you tell me what is going on," she seethed. "Where is J. W.?"

"He collapsed on the heels of some bad news I had to give him. The ambulance is here, and the paramedics suspect a heart attack, but he refuses to go with them until he talks with you about the fashion show!" The dark eyes held hers angrily. "It seems he thinks his executive designer can solve any problem."

"What problem is that?" she asked warily.

He hesitated before saying, "Clare L'aimant has disappeared. The wedding number will have to be eliminated from the show."

"*Eliminated?*" B. G. reeled from shock. "The wedding *is* the show! All the bridesmaids' gowns, the intimate apparel, the trousseau fashions—the entire show pivots around your wedding. The press has been primed for weeks to expect a storybook wedding at the design show of the century. You can't call off the wedding. You have to find Clare!"

"Precisely my father's reaction," Jordan said dryly. "You two are cut out of the same bolt of cloth." He steered her to the other door.

"Knowing Clare she's probably pulling a publicity stunt. She's been known to do it before," Bergitta offered hopefully.

He pushed open the door to his father's office. B. G. took one look at the ashen face of her elderly boss and went cold. Her eyes flickered across the sagging frame, taking in the labored breathing and dilated pupils.

"Hello, J. W.," she gulped. "I hear you're not feeling well."

Weakly, he raised his fist and thumped his chest. "It's the old pump, lying down on the job," he rasped hoarsely. He reached out and took B. G.'s hand, drawing her to his side. With a nod he dismissed the paramedics, then asked B. G. in a weakening voice, "Did Jordan tell you?"

Not giving B. G. a chance to answer, Jordan shifted uneasily, eyeing his father's condition with concern. "This doesn't have to be discussed now, Pop." He laid a reassuring hand on his shoulder. "Don't forget that I'm pretty resourceful, and I'm sure Ms. Blakely's creative genius extends beyond the sketch pad. Leave the design show to us. After you spend a couple of quiet days in the hospital you'll be as good as new. I suspect your symptoms are just caused by overwork."

Somehow Jordan had imperceptibly signaled the medics who returned and immediately began to transfer the elder Worthington from the office couch to the waiting stretcher. As they wheeled the patient toward a back stairway where the ambulance had arrived quietly to avoid alarming the staff, J.W. cast a pleading look at his favorite designer.

She squeezed the clammy hand. "Jordan is right. We'll see that the show is a success. After all, we've worked too hard to lose out at this late date. Just don't upstage us and capture the headlines," she teased with a grin. "We want positive attention from the press."

He attempted to return her smile. "Don't worry. I haven't reserved space in the obituary column yet." Then the paramedics wheeled him out and B. G. and Jordan were alone.

B. G. gripped the edge of the chair with white-knuckled intensity. "Look," she said tautly, "you really don't have any choice but to find your fiancée. Your father's health is at stake. The company's reputation is at stake. Every fashion magazine in the United States and abroad is covering us, not to mention buyers from all the major retailers—five hundred of them!"

Jordan dropped his muscular frame into his father's ample chair and pressed his fingertips together thoughtfully. "I'm well aware that Clare has put a colossal monkey wrench into the sensation of the season. On the other hand, it was not the swiftest of moves to plan an entire season around one limited line."

"If it happens to be the bridal season, it is a very smart move," she snapped, stung by the criticism. "Besides, I hardly think you're in a position to make a judgment when most of your time is spent jetting from continent to continent."

He looked at her coolly, his eyes traveling the length of her expertly tailored form, not missing the inherent

12

feminine sensuality camouflaged by her executive disguise. She colored under his gaze.

"We have more important things to do than indulge in pettiness," he said. "There are some fast decisions to be made." He picked up the phone and dialed his father's secretary.

"What are you going to do?" B. G. gasped, not expecting a decision quite *that* fast.

"I'm calling off the eleven-o'clock staff meeting and advising the fitters that Clare is late. That should give us time to get our bearings. And then I'm going to the hospital to see how Pop is doing."

"I'm coming with you."

He shrugged. "As you wish."

B. G. welcomed the biting February air. It somehow matched her mood. Once in the cab she stared unseeingly at the blackened heaps on either side of the street. They looked more like drooling coal piles than snow banks. This was the worst time of year to stay in New York. It was the time of year that the fortunate escaped to the Bahamas, or the more fortunate, to the Riviera. B. G. herself had planned a tropical vacation as soon as the show was over. Judging from the events of the last hour, however, the show might already be over. Morosely, she brooded over the loss of her big moment. It had taken five years to build, and like a sand castle, it was dissolving before her very eyes with one swift turn of the tide. She could have wept.

She turned to the stern-faced man sitting beside her. His square jaw was hard and immovable, and she suddenly noticed that the deep-set eyes and implacable countenance held character she had never credited him with before. She had seen him coming and going from board meetings at Design House, but she had seen him more in the pages of sports magazines and Sunday society sections where he was always scaling the Alps adventurously or surfing nine-foot waves in Hawaii. She found herself very curious about a woman who would

13

forsake this god of the media on the eve of their wedding.

"Are you absolutely certain Clare intends to miss her own wedding?" B. G. asked. Privately, she couldn't imagine the self-centered model's allowing anything to stand in the way of the international publicity she would receive from the event. It had been her idea to have the marriage vows exchanged as a part of the season's showing. B. G. remembered now that Jordan had never sanctioned those plans but had only gone along with them. She peered at him suspiciously.

"How did you discover your fiancée was missing?"

He answered absentmindedly without a trace of emotion, "When she didn't arrive on her scheduled flight from London last night."

"Then perhaps she was waylaid or missed her flight," B. G. suggested hopefully.

"Not a chance! Clare is a professional. She's accustomed to keeping airline schedules."

There was something odd here, the young designer realized. The prospective bridegroom was almost nonchalant about the disappearance.

"Aren't you worried about her?"

"Not especially. Clare can take care of herself."

B. G. probed further. "There is more to this than you're telling, isn't there?"

His silence confirmed her suspicion, but he offered no explanation. Suddenly B. G. was swamped with a wave of anger. Color mounted in her face.

"I see! Your autocratic position gives you the power to destroy a long and strenuous career, just like *that*!" She snapped her fingers. "Yet you owe no one an explanation, reason, or apology!"

"My father has had all three," he told her, unperturbed. "He accepts my apology."

"If he has accepted it, why is he lying in a hospital?"

"Because he takes this business too seriously," Jordan

14

said. "Design House will survive, wedding or no wedding."

B. G. grimaced. "It might not be quite that simple. If the show bombs, so will Design House."

Jordan's countenance hardened as though struck in stone.

"Whose idea was it to limit the line to nuptial wear?"

"What does it matter?" she countered, then grudgingly conceded. "The fashion board decided."

"Of which you are a member?"

"Of course!"

"Ah! I see. How clever of you to see to it that every design pointed to and enhanced your own personal creation. Possibly your best stroke of strategy in years. The wedding gown cannot possibly fail when the entire show has been orchestrated to crescendo at the *pièce de résistance*!"

"That's not fair and you know it!" B. G. cried. "If the gown is a success it will be because the design is superior, not because I have manipulated the show." She turned her head, determined that he would not see the tears that were stinging her eyes.

She came back to the subject of Clare's disappearance.

"I'll consider myself fortunate if the gown doesn't become a laughing stock caused by our 'mystery' bride who, it appears, is going to remain a mystery from now on." She laughed bitterly. "Boy! The press should have a field day with that one.

"This whole thing is a disaster. I doubt J. W. can survive it. He was counting on this show to—" She stopped short, as though protecting privileged information.

Jordan's quizzical glance scrutinized her. "Yes? Go on."

She masked her face with an impassive stare. "It's just that the show is very, very important—to both of us."

"Yes, I'm sure it is," he shot out. "Pop is an incurable

15

workaholic. He had no business starting in a field about which he knew nothing after he retired from a successful high-tech career." A brooding look clouded his eyes. "I suppose it was too much to expect him to stay retired. For him, work is the anesthetic that numbs the reality of life." Through narrowed eyes he scanned her figure from the smart but sensible black pumps to the severely knotted hairstyle that lent a patrician elegance to her delicate features.

"I suspect, Ms. Blakely, that you are the female counterpart of the hard-driving male executive, right down to those atrocious initials you use as a substitute for a name!"

Anger raked up and down B. G.'s spine like fiery porcupine quills. "At least I'm not bumming around the beaches and ski slopes of the world like some overgrown baby who has worn out his playpen!" she snapped.

His straight, hooded eyebrows shot up, unveiling a stern but not unkind look. "You don't know what you're talking about, Ms. Blakely," he said flatly. Then suddenly his eyes twinkled, and he leaned over, deliberately locking her glance into his own piercing stare. He laughed. "Ah, yes! I do indeed glimpse a green-eyed monster lurking in the shadows of those gorgeous, dark eyes." She gasped at his audacity when he removed the horn-rimmed spectacles from her face and looked deeper into her eyes.

"Let me hazard a guess that you have not so much as taken your standard 'two weeks with pay' to visit relatives and renew schoolgirl friendships—hmmmmm?"

B. G. blushed furiously. Not for the world would she admit how accurately he had summed up her addiction to the security of a work routine. She tossed her head defiantly. "How did this conversation cross over into my personal life?" she demanded. "If you are quite sure your fiancée isn't playing games with us in hopes of some extra press exposure, then we need to be putting

16

our energies into some serious discussion about how we are to compensate for the sudden absence of the bride at the wedding finale."

He said quietly, "I can assure you that Clare is not playing games. Now, perhaps you had better brief me on the general status of the show so I can make some qualified decisions."

For the next few minutes B. G. brought him up to date on the publicity that had been released. Editors from every major newspaper and fashion magazine were already en route and would arrive early to get exclusive interviews with the principals. Store buyers from both sides of the Atlantic had reservations, and several major television talk-show appearances had been arranged by the marketing department. She pointed out the commercial loss that would result were the show to be canceled, and the credibility of the company would suffer an irrevocable setback if the wedding did not materialize.

"Entire issues of women's magazines have been reserved for this story, so it is not only our business that will be affected, but the publishing industry as well. I would hate to make an enemy of them. At best, we would come off the laughing stock of the fashion world."

Jordan nodded slowly as he began to grasp the widespread ramifications of a precipitously canceled wedding that had been billed as the fashion event of the season. Having been abroad for the past several months, he had been unaware of all the elaborate preparations.

Seeing that she had made some inroads into his perception of the problem, B. G. pressed her point further. "The company has been in financial reversal for some time. That's one of the reasons for your father's poor health. If we should lose him, that, combined with a flop of the show, will pretty well take the company down for the third time—and with it will go the jobs of the breadwinners whose families depend on us for their livelihood."

A slightly scornful smile crossed his face. "Come now, Ms. Blakely, let's keep our perspective. It's not the jobs of others you are most concerned about. It's your own career that stands to lose the most, is it not? Well, you can rest your fears. I am convinced that it would be more than an inconvenience to cancel the show at this point. It would constitute a breach of trust with our long-standing customers. It is also quite plain to me that the wedding unfortunately *is* the show. So I'll see to it that the wedding comes off as scheduled."

B. G. heaved a sigh of relief. "Then you will manage to find Clare immediately? Final fittings were scheduled for today, and the media is pressing us to release the identity of our 'mystery bride.' "

"You didn't properly understand me," he said, assuming an air of patience. "I know Clare's whereabouts. It is *this* fashion scene she has disappeared from, not our relationship. You will have to accept the fact that she cannot fulfill her commitment. Take my word for it. Her appearance at this time would be more of a liability to the company's reputation than her disappearance."

The positive authority with which he spoke left no doubt in B. G.'s mind that he knew what he was talking about. She lifted her hands in a helpless gesture.

"Then I don't understand. How can the wedding come off as scheduled?"

He explained, "Since the identity of the bride has not yet been announced, we will simply fill the role with someone suitable."

B. G. considered the possibility thoughtfully as she gazed at the blur of street vendors, policemen, and shoppers who crowded the New York thoroughfare.

She shook her head. "I can't see that it would work. A phony wedding would just make a mockery of our original plans."

"I wasn't contemplating a mock ceremony. Of course the wedding would have to be the real thing in order to deliver what we promised."

"You mean you would find a stand-in bride?" B. G. queried, as she slowly comprehended. "The press is expecting a well-known personality. You can hardly pick someone off the street. Besides we could never trust just anyone to keep our confidence. Credibility has to be impeccable; otherwise, the entire publicity campaign might as well be scrubbed."

"Agreed on all points, Ms. Blakely, but I daresay we could trust ourselves with this little charade—right?"

B. G. looked at him blankly, trying to discern his meaning.

He continued, "What could fill the hungry jaws of the press better than a good old-fashioned 'rags to riches' storybook wedding? I can see the headlines now: 'Fashion Designer Moves to Top Ranks—Weds President-Elect of Design House Board.' "

After the full meaning of his words had sunk in, she retorted, "But I'm *not* the firm's top designer, nor are you the president-elect!"

He shouted with laughter. "That was hardly the reply I expected to my proposal, Ms. Blakely!"

"And I can assure you that was hardly the proposal I expected to solve this problem. It was a bad joke." She rolled her eyes scornfully. "Get serious!"

He sobered quickly. "I was entirely serious. The plan would work, and as soon as the purpose was served, the marriage would, of course, be annulled. My father has requested that I replace him as president, which I intend to do just long enough to get the company in a stable financial position again. All this could mesh very well."

"B-but part of the advertising campaign is the two-month European cruise to photograph the trousseau fashions," she objected.

"Right. That would certainly have to be a part of the plan."

B. G. shook her head as though this were all part of a bad dream. "I couldn't be away from work that long."

"You could if I mandated it."

The seriousness with which he was proceeding alarmed her. She could almost feel a steel trap closing on her.

The cab turned the corner of the block where the hospital was located. As it began to slow, Jordan said, "Think it over, Ms. Blakely. A few weeks of inconvenience is a small price to pay in return for your design career. There could be other rewards as well," he winked enigmatically.

She looked at him askance, wondering at his meaning and waiting for him to enlighten her.

"I'm sure my influence could ensure an appointment to the Board of Directors for you. I'm surprised there hasn't been a woman appointed before now." He saw the gleam in her eyes and smiled smugly. "I thought that would guarantee your interest," he gloated as the cab pulled to a stop beside the hospital curb. "And of course you would earn a handsome bonus for dedication above and beyond the call of duty. So you see? You could just consider this part of your work. *That* should make it easy for you."

Jordan alighted and helped B. G. onto the pavement. Immediately they were surrounded by cameras. He muttered something unintelligible about ambulance-chasing reporters and gave them as little information as possible, promising a detailed report as soon as the doctor had made a diagnosis. He casually declared that the mild discomfort his father was suffering could no doubt be attributed to the flu. B. G. marveled at his skill in handling the press and grinned at the poker face he presented.

A persistent reporter from *Women's Wear Daily* kept pace with them as they pushed their way to the hospital door. She shoved a microphone into Jordan's face. "Mr. Worthington, will this affect your wedding plans for Thursday?"

He smiled cheerfully. "Most assuredly not. The wedding will go on as planned."

"When will we know the identity of the bride?" the reporter persisted.

In a surprise action, Jordan drew B. G. affectionately into the circle of his arm and bestowed a proud, beaming smile upon her.

"Shall we tell them now, darling?" He pressed his mouth against her ear to feign an endearment but used the moment to whisper, "What in thunder do those initials stand for?"

"Bergitta," she gulped in a whisper.

He turned to the reporter. "You journalists don't miss a thing, so you probably already know that Bergitta and I have known each other a long time. I'm surprised you haven't already guessed our good news," he smiled engagingly. "At present she is a promising designer on my father's staff at Design House, but I'm soon going to take her away from all that." The gleam of ardor in his eyes would have won an Oscar. "Bergitta and I will be married on Thursday. She will wear the wedding dress she designed for herself," he lied glibly, giving every impression that he was thoroughly enjoying the adventure. "After that, we will honeymoon abroad, traveling in Europe and on the continent." He waited as the astounded reporter feverishly changed the tape in her recorder. Then he concluded the interview by saying, "When we return, I will take up the reins of the company at my father's request."

Bergitta was too stunned to do anything but gape at him until she caught his eye signals and obligingly smiled for the camera.

The reporter's gaze narrowed shrewdly. "It was rumored that Clare L'aimant was listed on the printer's program as the bride-elect."

Bergitta groaned inwardly, wondering how Jordan would dodge this.

"Ah yes," he said. "Clare is a good friend of both Bergitta's and mine. She graciously agreed to model one of the fashions. No doubt her name was printed on the wrong line of the program. It's unfortunate that an illness will keep her from participating after all." Bergitta was stunned by his quick maneuvering. Of course, he had had plenty of experience. It was becoming apparent that she had greatly underestimated this man who had just commandeered the situation and had it firmly under control.

When the reporters had gone at last, she wheeled on him.

"You might at least have given me the chance to refuse your proposal! It seems to me you took a lot for granted."

He shrugged his shoulders. "It's called calculated bargaining. Each of us has something to offer the other. I believe the appropriate phrase is 'negotiating a business deal.' "

Bergitta looked at him coldly. "Do you really imagine you engaged my services as your wife in exchange for a bonus and a position on the board?"

His smile was smooth and tolerant, and suddenly Bergitta saw how she must look from his point of view. If she went through with this she would have to put up with his insufferable opinion that she was a calculating female, who would use even the sacred rites of marriage to further her career. If she didn't go through with it, the company would suffer, and even more importantly, employees who had been loyal for many years would also suffer.

She followed Jordan into the elevator, quietly thoughtful. Upstairs in J. W.'s room the doctor beckoned Jordan outside for a private consultation, and Bergitta was left to break the news. "It's my fault you're caught in this trap," J. W. said.

22

"Nonsense," Bergitta chided. "How could it be your fault? All you did was give me a great opportunity in the design business. I'll always be grateful for that." She kept her voice light, not wanting to alarm the deathly sick man by showing any anxiety about the alternative wedding plan.

J. W. grunted discontentedly, "I don't know what got into that fickle-minded dame, Clare. Never did like her. And Jordan should have kept in closer touch with us. He must have had some idea that things were going sour between them."

"I don't think we can blame anyone," Bergitta pointed out. "Besides, Jordan doesn't seem unduly concerned about Clare's failure to show up, so I don't think we need to waste our energies on his and Clare's problems. In fact," she said musingly, "he seems almost relieved."

J. W. sighed and fell back against the pillows on his hospital bed. "He's not the only one. I dreaded the thought of having that egotistical creature in the family."

He caught the soft, tapered hand that was smoothing his bedcover and looked at Bergitta wistfully. "If Jordan had any sense, he would look for someone steady and with her feet on the ground—someone like yourself." His voice took on a hopeful tone. "I wish there could be something real and lasting in this marriage between you and Jordan."

She smiled kindly. "I'm afraid that could never happen, J. W. This relationship will be strictly business."

"That's what I thought you would say," he nodded acceptingly. "That being the case, there will be more than adequate compensation for your cooperation."

"The opportunity to show my designs is compensation enough, J. W. You assigned me to coordinate the show, and I'm just doing my job—even if the means to bring it off did turn out to be somewhat unorthodox," she grinned, trying to cover the churning turmoil inside her.

"That's the attitude that makes you a pro, B. G.," her boss smiled, just as his son returned with the doctor.

The test results were not as bad as they had figured. J. W. had suffered a mild heart attack, but the doctor warned him that continued stress would have more dangerous consequences.

Bergitta and Jordan locked knowing glances. The warning made it doubly imperative for the design show to succeed. J. W.'s life could be at stake.

Chapter Two

From that moment on Jordan took over. He seemed to
sense the shock reaction Bergitta was feeling from the
spinning events of the morning. At 7:55 a.m. Bergitta
had gone to work expecting to conduct final briefings
with the bride-elect. At 11:55 a.m. she *was* the bride-
elect. After they had applied for blood tests and a marriage license, Jordan noticed her wan appearance and
suggested lunch. But she shook her head, suddenly
feeling nauseous at the very thought of food.

Jordan directed the taxi driver to a restaurant anyway,
the Skyway, which revolved on the top of a high-rise
hotel and gave a lofty view of New York City.

A cocktail waitress appeared to take their order for
drinks. Bergitta hesitated. She never drank, but if there
were ever a time she felt the need for a stiff drink, it was
now!

However, Jordan unhesitatingly answered, "Nothing
for either of us, thanks."

Bergitta's deep, dark eyes swept him in surprise.
From the lifestyle he led, she would have thought he
never missed an opportunity. He began to make sugges-
tions from the menu. She ordered a party chicken salad
soufflé made with whipped cream and grapes. Jordan
chose his standard favorite of steak and oysters broiled
in a special piquant sauce.

They watched through the large plate glass windows as the scenes changed slowly. The Statue of Liberty in the New York Harbor came into view, and minutes later the Empire State Building made its appearance.

Jordan lifted his glass of Perrier in a mock salute. "An appropriate place to celebrate your pinnacle of success, wouldn't you say?"

"I never celebrate success prematurely. It doesn't pay to take public acceptance for granted," Bergitta disclaimed.

His gaze pierced her. "There are some who would claim your biggest success is your marriage to the president of the board."

She sniffed. "There are also some who claim the moon is made of cheese, but I don't agree with them either."

He laughed outright with deep full tones, and something about his genuine delight at her answer attracted her. His laugh had an irresistible little-boy quality about it.

After that, he conducted business just as though this were any business lunch. His first order of business was to relieve Bergitta of the coordinating responsibilities for the show, freeing her time to fill Clare's appointments with the media. Bergitta regretted not being able to follow through with the floral designer and the choreographer as she had planned, but she knew Jordan's decision was the right one.

Jordan outlined the next few days, establishing his role as acting president in his father's absence. It felt strange to be answering suddenly to someone whom she had never considered an integral part of the Design House team. He surprised her with more knowledge about the business than she would have thought possible given his rare attendance at board meetings.

They went over the details of the honeymoon that would take them to all parts of Europe aboard his private yacht. Chris Jamison, who normally handled all of

Clare's publicity photographs, would be accompanying them to send pictures of the trousseau designs back to the fashion slicks. The marketing department hoped to boost sales and keep the buyers interested by showing them the fashions in exotic locations around the world.

After the technicalities of the next few days were prioritized and their meal was finished, Jordan settled back to enjoy a favorite European coffee. His eyes slid lazily over Bergitta, assessing her attributes.

"Tell me about yourself," he said unexpectedly. "I don't want to be caught off guard should some inquiring reporter be interested enough in our announcement to probe for details. For instance, where were you born, which college did you graduate from, do you have brothers and sisters, and how did you happen to become a designer? That question is sure to be asked!"

Bergitta made a wry face. "You won't find much that's newsworthy in my past. I grew up in the cornfields and cow pastures of Iowa. We went into the big city of Des Moines once a year if we could afford it."

"I can't quite picture you in blue-checked gingham with a milk pail on your arm." Merriment flickered in Jordan's deep-set brown eyes. "I take it your father was a farmer?"

Bergitta bit her lip as though reluctant to answer. "No," she said slowly, "he was a minister. I grew up in a parsonage."

"I see," Jordan said, startled. He began to study her like a curio. "I don't believe I have ever met anyone from that, er..."

"Most people here in New York haven't," she volunteered. "But in Iowa, everything from business to pleasure revolves around church."

Again his eyes surveyed her sophisticated loveliness, which he connected with the fine business mind he had come to respect these last few hours.

"How did you get from there to here?"

"I can't imagine you will be asked that question," she objected.

"You would be surprised. The press can be relentless in their pursuit of a good story."

She took a deep breath and allowed her mind to wander back in time. "I suppose my father's profession inadvertently had something to do with my own profession," she admitted.

"That seems an unlikely development," Jordan commented, becoming more interested. "Go on."

"He did not pastor the 'high-steepled churches' as I used to call them when I was a girl," she smiled. "He pioneered churches in farm communities where there was no place to worship. Those were hard times, because there was no established congregation to pay a salary and provide a house. Of course, that meant there was also no money for pretty clothes. My mother was an expert seamstress, and when I was tiny she dressed me from the remnant table at Woolworth's." Bergitta smiled wistfully. "I can still see her sitting up late on Saturday night to finish a hem and sew on the buttons. I was the best-dressed girl in my Sunday school class, and all the others were jealous," she laughed, remembering.

"I was proud of those clothes because they were the only things I had that were as good as what someone else had. Then, when I was older and we had settled in one town, I began to study fashion magazines at the library and sketched out ideas for Mom to sew, always adding a touch of my own here and there—especially with detail."

Jordan nodded. "I hear that your talents lie in giving great detail to a design."

"Without it, a design is worthless as far as I am concerned," she said, and she continued her story. "Once the local Woman's Club asked me to design an entire fashion show for a charity luncheon. My designs were well received, and that's when I began to realize that maybe I had something special." She stopped speaking as though hindered by a thought.

"Then did you go on to college to major in fashion design?"

"No." A note of bitterness crept into her voice. "My father wanted me to become a school teacher. I finished high school a year early and won a scholarship with my high grades. By that time, my father's church had grown, and with my part-time job, there was enough money to pay personal expenses. I got all the way to my senior year. Then he lost his church and was no longer able to help."

Jordan looked puzzled. "How do you 'lose' a church? You make it sound as though he misplaced it."

Bergitta smiled at his humor but answered soberly, "No, he didn't misplace his church. He may have misplaced his priorities, though. He and my mother spent all their energies establishing the congregation and putting up a new church building. They even neglected their own personal well-being. They did such a good job that the pastorate became attractive to other pastors who 'courted' the congregation. Before my father realized what was happening, political strings had been pulled in the church, and my father was replaced after ten years of dedication. This happened two weeks before they were to move into a new parsonage the church had built. It would have been the first decent home my mother had ever had.

"I had just entered my senior year, and needless to say, I was very upset. Being an only child, I was very close to my parents. I wanted my father to fight to keep what he had worked for, but he refused to be a part of church politics. I felt he was being unfair to my mother, and besides that, there was a big row because I had changed my major to fashion design without telling him. During all the brouhaha my grades went down and I lost my scholarship. My father was given another small church to build and, of course, he could not afford my tuition. 29

"You poor kid," Jordan sympathized. "How did you finally make it to New York?"

Bergitta bristled. She had been poor all her life and had worked hard to overcome the image. She tilted her chin and retorted, "A recruiter from Design House was smart enough to recognize my potential when he visited the campus at the end of my junior year. He got J. W. to look over my portfolio, and they brought me to New York to apprentice. I completed my senior year at night school. J.W. was kind enough to underwrite my expenses."

There was silence between them. "You're still bitter about your father's poor judgment, aren't you?"

"Does it show?"

"Of course." He turned the coffee cup back and forth in his hand, deeply thoughtful. "There is politics in everything, Bergitta, and the design business is the world's worst political arena. If you want to get ahead, you have to be professional enough to handle it. From what I understand, you've had your own power struggles within the company."

"Yes, and I am well aware that some of the other designers feel I've finagled my way into J. W.'s respect and confidence because I've worked hard. Nothing is more important than my career, and he has always known he could rely on me to meet deadlines whatever had to suffer in my personal life."

His direct gaze connected with hers. "Then I take it there are no serious suitors in your life who could cause embarrassment or otherwise complicate plans for this marriage?"

"No, none."

The restaurant had revolved to a magnificent view of the New York skyline. Bergitta swept a graceful arm toward the mass of silver-gray steel, now struck with noonday sunlight.

"They call this the 'Big Apple,' " she said. "I decided a long time ago that I would have my bite of the apple— the biggest one I could get!"

Jordan placed his Diner's Club card on the check the waitress had brought, and answered with a shrug of his shoulders. "If that's what you want, then I say 'go for it.' Just be careful that your bite doesn't choke you."

Bergitta sat at the dressing table of her small but elegant apartment. She drew a brush through her tresses, shorter now since the make-over artist assigned to her had snipped them into a becoming style that framed her face but they were still long enough to be twined into a fashionable crown, which she felt the wedding dress and veil called for. Gone, too, were the glasses. Jordan had figured out that they were only a part of an unconscious business disguise and had pocketed them, explaining that they didn't exactly fit her new role.

Bergitta was surprised at how smoothly things had gone the last two days. She and Jordan had barely made it back to the office in time to call a staff meeting and make their announcement before the evening papers broke the story. There had been cheers and applause, from the stockroom clerks to the department heads, for Bergitta and Jordan were both popular among the personnel. It had been rumored that Clare would be the lucky lady to snare the boss's son; so, much of the excitement was generated by the element of surprise.

Libby, the seamstress, had laughed good-naturedly when Bergitta reported late that afternoon for final fittings. "I should have guessed the truth at the first fittings when you said you were only standing in for the bride," she had said through a mouthful of pins. The truth of the matter was, Bergitta *had* been standing in for Clare, but she had smiled and let Libby think what she might.

The hours had raced by, and now only one more day remained. She stared at her reflection in the mirror and put down her brush. This time tomorrow evening she would be Mrs. Jordan Wright Worthington III. She swallowed hard, still not certain this was all happening. She began to apply a frothy whipped foundation to her already smooth skin with light even strokes.

Her mind traveled back over the years, recalling the high hopes for romance she had once had. At sixteen years old, she had fantasized an adoring bridegroom awaiting her at a candlelit altar, caressing her with his eyes as she drifted down the aisle in satin and lace. Together they would dedicate themselves with solemn vows to God, and they would plan their lives to glorify their heavenly Father.

She blotted the foundation. What had happened to the dream? Had she sacrificed all that was sacred on the altar of another dream: *success*? Were Jordan's implications accurate after all? Had the success mania gripped her in its vise to the exclusion of all else?

She picked up the make-up palette and began to add a glittered eye shadow. Her lusterless, brooding eyes needed the sparkle.

Her image in the mirror stared back at her, hollow-cheeked and ashen. She wished she didn't have to go to the family dinner party Jordan's parents were having this evening, nor to the staff reception that was to follow at the old Waldorf-Astoria. She hated this deception! Tears sprang to her eyes, and the thought of chucking the whole thing—career and company—momentarily flashed through her mind.

The doorbell rang. It was probably Jordan. He had gone to the airport to pick up her parents. He played the part of the obliging bridegroom well, she thought wryly, as she deftly wriggled into a swath of pale green silk.

She tripped up the two steps to the entrance landing with a lighter tread than she felt and plastered a bright smile on her face. Her parents had gallantly gone along with the last-minute wedding plans. Bergitta had not tried to answer the unspoken questions posed by their long silences as she had hurriedly fabricated a story to justify the sudden marriage. She knew that they were not fooled, and she had promised to explain more later. They had fallen in with the last minute plans and were now here to play their traditional roles in a non-traditional wedding.

She swung open the door and flew into her mother's arms, feeling more like a lost little girl than ever before. Her father reached over and patted her shoulder with one hand while blowing his emotions into a flag-sized handkerchief with the other. He scrutinized her countenance, concluded that his daughter badly needed rest, and admonished his future son-in-law to see that she got it. Bergitta blushed, but Jordan nodded and charmingly agreed that his bride must relax the minute they boarded the yacht for their honeymoon cruise. He even dropped a kiss on her lips to convey the sincerity of his sentiments.

"That wasn't necessary," she hissed when her mother and father went to the bedroom to unpack.

He laughed at her discomfiture. "You'd better get used to it. This is just the beginning of a long evening in which we both have to be convincingly ardent lovers."

The knowledge that he was right only made her angrier. She stamped into the bedroom.

Her mother's dress, which Libby had stitched together at the last minute from Bergitta's design, was spread across the bed. She had chosen the gray wispy fabric shot with silver, with her mother's silver curls in mind. She marveled that her mother's measurements never changed. The dress fit her divinely.

As Bergitta helped her mother dress for dinner, Mrs. Blakely chattered happily, her conversation punctuated here and there with a purposeful question dropped casually into the talk. Bergitta adroitly evaded the questions while privately wishing she could tell her mother everything. She respected her parents and, except for not telling her father she had changed her major, she had always tried to be honest with them. They had taught her that truth was better than gold.

There it was again. That niggling idea that she had traded her personal values for wealth and professional status. It bothered her so much that she sighed and began to twist a loose curl around her index finger—a symptom her mother understood well.

"What is it, dear?" Mrs. Blakely asked. "What's wrong?"

"Why, nothing, Mother," Bergitta feigned innocence. "Why would you think anything is wrong?"

"I know a happy bride when I see one—and I don't see one." Her mother's direct gaze descended on her daughter's plastic smile.

"Why the rush, Bergitta? You said on the phone you would explain later. Is there some reason you must proceed with such haste?" Hurt tinged the mother's tender lips.

"Oh, Mother! I know what you're thinking, but it's nothing like that! It's just that—well, it seemed a good idea to include the ceremony in the fashion show since I designed the wedding dress. A wedding is a novel way to introduce a whole new line of wedding attire, wouldn't you say?"

"So that's it! You've commercialized the most sacred event of a lifetime."

"Please, Mother! Let's not argue. I know you have never approved of my dedication to this career, but it is *my* life!" Her mother's lips trembled. "So it is, Bergitta. It is your life that your father and I gave to you. We tried to equip you with values and goals that would help you keep a balanced perspective about what is important in life. But you have turned your career into a god, Bergitta."

"You don't understand, Mother. Please try to believe, in spite of all your doubts, that I'm doing what I have to do. I love you and Daddy more than anything in the world, but I have to do what's right for me."

With a tap at the door, Jordan urged them to hurry. Bergitta gathered up the white mink Jordan had sent over from the most exclusive furrier in New York. He had said it was a wedding present, but Bergitta suspected he had simply supplied it as a status symbol appropriate for the event, just as he had provided the engagement ring. She glanced down at her left hand. What an unusual ring he had chosen. The two-carat, emerald-cut diamond was attached to the gold circlet at one end and the rest of the stone extended almost to her knuckle. She was sure he would write it all off as a business expense.

Write it off, Bergitta mocked silently. That's what they were doing with this whole phony marriage— writing off the confidence and trust of everyone associated with Design House. She leaned over to pat a final dusting of powder on her face and stared angrily at the young woman in the mirror. She had let herself down.

Jordan placed the mink wrap around her shoulders with polished smoothness. Her breath came more quickly as he gently fastened the catch at her throat. She was fascinated by his hands. They were strong, yet they moved deftly and quickly at anything he did.

Riding to the suburbs where Jordan's parents lived, she listened with scant amusement as her father tactfully tried to find out Jordan's line of work, and Jordan just as tactfully skirted the subject, explaining he would temporarily act as head of Design House. Bergitta wanted to scream, *He doesn't have a line of work, Father! He's a taker, not a giver!*

A woman young for her years welcomed them at the Worthingtons. "Black slink" was the only way to describe how she was dressed, Bergitta decided.

"Hello, Beryl," Jordan greeted her. She seemed far too young to be the mother of this thirty-two year old playboy. Confirming this, Jordan introduced her to Bergitta's parents as his "wicked old stepmother," a title more just than jest judging from the sparks of hostility flying between them.

She felt rather than saw Beryl sizing up her appearance as she went into the parlor to greet J. W. who was resting by the fire. He had been released from the hospital only hours before, with stiff admonitions from the doctor to take it easy.

Dinner was an awkward affair. Jordan had not told Beryl the real circumstances behind the marriage because, he explained to Bergitta, she was a "vapor-head"; everything that went into her head came out again in a changed form. Beryl had insisted on following through with the dinner despite J. W.'s illness, and he was putting forth great effort to cope with the occasion. Bergitta felt sorry for him.

Toasts were made, and once again Bergitta was surprised that their glasses were filled with a sparkling white grape juice. Only Beryl had insisted on being served champagne. Was the abstinence out of deference to her parents or perhaps because the doctor had forbidden J. W.'s using alcohol?

Beryl began a babbling monologue about romance, hailing the developed sensual powers of older men as preferable to the inexperience of younger ones. "Of course, I hardly think you will find Jordan inexperienced, Bergitta," the blonde woman winked broadly.

Bergitta blushed out of embarrassment for her parents, and Jordan drew in his breath sharply at the tasteless remark. Fortunately, the phone rang, sparing them further unpleasantness, or so Bergitta thought, until Beryl returned to the dining room with a saccharin smile and announced that Clare was on the phone to speak with Jordan.

He muttered an expletive and had the presence of mind to excuse himself to Bergitta. "You don't mind, do you, dear?" he questioned solicitously.

"Of course not," she said promptly. "Go right ahead."

Bergitta was just about to change the subject before

her parents could wonder who Clare was, when Beryl took it upon herself to explain.

"Clare is just about my very best friend in the whole world," she gushed. "It really is too bad that the romance thing didn't work out between Clare and Jordan, but these lovers' quarrels do happen." She reached over and patted Bergitta on the arm. "I'm sure you will help him forget all about her."

Mrs. Blakely's eyes darkened, and her father scowled, squinting at his daughter closely as though searching for some reason for this peculiar situation.

Thus Jordan returned to the table to find them in suspended animation, no one knowing what to do or say next.

"I think we must forego dessert if we are to be on time for the reception the staff is giving for us," Jordan smiled at Bergitta.

There was a sigh of relief as the party made a hasty exit from the table.

Bergitta was helping her mother locate her wrap in the hall closet when she heard Jordan speaking in hushed tones to Beryl. "It really isn't necessary for you to come tonight since my father won't be there. He needs someone here with him."

"Nonsense!" Beryl protested, giving her platinum head a toss. "The doctors didn't say he needed constant care."

"How would you know? You never even went to the hospital."

"You don't know. Perhaps I came after you had already left."

"I checked." His voice was seething.

For an answer, Beryl stalked to the closet, yanked her seal-skin from the hanger and thrust it into Jordan's hands. His icy expression chilled Bergitta to the bone as she watched him help his father's wife into her wrap. Did she imagine it, or had his viselike fingers gripped Beryl's shoulders with tensile strength when he turned her toward the parlor to say good night to J. W.?

On the way into town, the party was silent, everyone lost in his or her own thoughts. Bergitta wondered what Clare had wanted. Judging from Jordan's cheerful demeanor when he returned to the room, the exchange must have been pleasant. He had made no explanation, nor did she expect him to. She had no claims whatsoever during this temporary arrangement.

Jordan concentrated on his driving, but the white knuckles clenched around the steering wheel were a dead giveaway that all was not as calm as his bland expression would imply. *Had* Clare upset him, or was he still angry with his stepmother, or was the phony wedding finally getting to him, too? Bergitta realized it probably was a combination of all three, and she stole a glance at the hard jawline of his stony countenance. Just to see him like this made her skin prickle.

Then reality dawned on her. She would spend the next few months of her life with this man and would learn all his moods. This was just the beginning. She sighed as she slumped back against the seat.

At the Waldorf the liveried doorman opened the door for her while a parking attendant went around to the driver's seat. Jordan's hand was under her elbow as they preceded the rest of the group to the ballroom. The orchestra struck a drum roll as they entered and accompanied the cheering crowd with crescendoing chords. Streamers and confetti showered Jordan and Bergitta, and she felt his arm tighten around her in a signal for her to greet the company. She began to wave as he was doing. The noise subsided as the orchestra drifted into a melodic refrain that blended with joyful sounds of the well-wishers as Jordan and Bergitta mingled with the crowd. Now and then Jordan steered her clear of a jostling elbow with a firm hand to her back or swept his arm about her shoulders as he introduced her to an acquaintance. Always she was aware of his touch and was startled to notice an unbidden chemistry between them. Although she couldn't say why, she knew that the awareness was there for him, too. Once during a brief intermission from the endless groups of congratulators, Jordan pulled her into his arms. He murmured huskily, "Time to do a little convincing." His lips found hers and touched them, then deepened the kiss into a fullness.

She pulled back, vaguely aware that those around were casting them sidelong glances.

Jordan raised an eyebrow. "Problem?"

"You don't have to be *that* convincing," she said, her breath coming in short spurts.

He laughed softly and pulled her back into a close embrace. "Maybe I'm the one who's being convinced," he whispered, his warm breath teasing her ear. "Without the armor of your executive image, you are a beautiful young woman, Bergitta." He dropped a kiss on her full, caressable lips. Her long lashes fluttered open, and she was trembling from the impact of his light kiss. "I think I'd like some punch now."

"Of course," he agreed unhesitatingly, and he led her to the refreshment table, stopping to chat with friends along the way. Other than business associates and Design House employees, many of Jordan's personal friends had been invited some weeks ago with a promise that they would meet the mystery bride on this evening. *I'm a mystery, all right,* Bergitta thought, enduring the stares piercing their polite masks. *They know I'm not Jordan's type.*

"This is good," she said to him, taking a sip of her punch. "Do you know what's in it?"

"Yes. Pineapple juice, tonic water, and a hint of mint—my own request." He motioned his glass toward the other side of the room. "There's a bar if you care to indulge."

"No, thanks. I'm fine. In fact, what I would really like is a glass of water. I'm parched."

Jordan motioned for the wine steward and gave him

39

the order for two glasses of Perrier.

For the first time, Bergitta had a chance to appreciate fully the magnificent ballroom of the Waldorf-Astoria which had been restored to the Edwardian time period. Mauve velvet love seats and couches were grouped on burgandy carpets scattered about the glistening wood floors, and each grouping was completed with marble tables and huge potted palms. The cream silk walls decorated with heavy, cream brocaded curtains, bore old-fashioned portraits in ornate, gilt frames.

"Like it?" Jordan inquired.

"It's stunning," she breathed, studying the crystal chandeliers hung from the scrolled plaster ceiling. "It's not exactly what I would choose to surround myself with the rest of my life, but it's perfect for an occasion like this."

He regarded her pensively. "And what is your taste in furnishings?" Then he suddenly held up a hand to hold back her answer. "No, let me guess." He folded his arms across his chest and concentrated his gaze on her. "You would be into fabrics, I think. Functional style would be as important to you as aesthetic appeal—am I right?"

"Right!" she laughed. "I'm afraid I'm a creature of comfort first and beauty second. It even shows up in the clothes I design. They must be functional first and move easily in the setting they are designed for, and then they must be attractive enough that their practicality doesn't show."

"You're never very far from your work, are you?" he smiled indulgently.

A fanfare sounded just as the wine steward delivered the two glasses to Jordan and Bergitta. They found themselves surrounded by several members of the board of directors who escorted them to a raised platform at the end of the room.

The board members presented them with an elegant sterling silver tea service on behalf of everyone at Design House, and Bergitta was touched by the sincere

40

pledge of devotion it represented. Jordan made a humorous, yet warm acceptance speech, after which Bergitta smiled at the crowd and raised her glass, calling, *"Hear, hear!"*

Someone from the crowd yelled, "Forget the speeches, Jordan. Show us some action!"

Jordan laughed and swept Bergitta into his arms. Still holding her glass, she placed her arms on his shoulders to control the distance between them. He sought and captivated her lips with a gentle press to appease the fun-loving crowd. Taking his cue from their cheers, he deepened his kiss to an intensity that suddenly had nothing to do with play-acting. It was as though the two of them were alone in the room, and Jordan's onslaught became intimately passionate. She suddenly realized he was giving her a message. He planned to take every legal advantage due him in their marriage! His signal that he would pursue physical intimacy with her was loud and clear.

Bergitta's thoughts raced swiftly. She couldn't fight him off and make a public scene. On the other hand, she dared not let him get by with his display. She must get her own message across. Suddenly, an ingenious idea occurred to her. She stretched her arms around his neck, seemingly to close the embrace, then tipped the glass and let the cold Perrier trickle down his collar.

His reaction was instantaneous. He thrust her from him.

"Sorry," she smiled demurely. "The glass slipped."

His arm was like a steel band around her waist, communicating his outrage to her, but his voice was tightly controlled as he bade the well-wishers good night, explaining that he wanted his bride to turn in early and get a good night's sleep! The slightly tipsy celebrators went wild at his implication, made doubly funny by Bergitta's blushing discomfort.

The ride home was silent. This was a world her parents knew nothing about. Therefore they made no comment on the evening. Beryl seemed preoccupied by the passing scenery, and Jordan was too coldly furious to attempt conversation. Uneasily, Bergitta suspected she would pay a price for her little caper.

Later, cuddled in her bathrobe, she dug her toes into the deep pile of the white carpet in her apartment and enjoyed the cup of herbal tea her mother had made for her. She was exhausted and longed to have a few days of rest here in this cozy refuge she had created for herself. She had chosen mural-sized contemporary paintings in splashes of yellow, orange, and gold to widen the walls of the tiny living room, and accent pillows repeated the colors in the paintings. She made a mental note to have the weekly cleaning service water her hanging ferns and airplane plants while she was away.

After they had dressed for bed, her mother and father came into the room and chatted a little while. Then Bergitta went into her peach and cream bedroom and turned down the beige satin spread for her parents.

Her mother offered to help her pack, but Bergitta said she was too tired and preferred to do it the next day. In the past forty-eight hours she had managed to snatch only five hours of sleep. Tonight she *must* get some rest! She kissed her parents good night, but she regretted that she could not keep her eyes open for a nice long visit.

As she relaxed at last on the sofa bed, she saw the full moon against the New York skyline, and her last conscious thought was that tomorrow night she would view that moon from the high seas.

When the buzzer on the alarm went off, Bergitta groaned and rolled over. It couldn't be morning already. She had barely closed her eyes! She groped for the button to shut off the noise and then realized in the darkness the clock wasn't buzzing at all. The illuminated hands pointed to two a.m.

The buzzing stopped and was followed by a light tapping at the front door. She stumbled across the room peered through the crack allowed by the night latch.

"Jordan!" she hissed. "What in the world are you doing here?"

He was leaning casually against the door jamb. "I came to wish you a happy wedding day." He pushed on the door slightly. "Open up. We have some unfinished business to take care of."

"You can't come in here. My parents are already asleep," she sputtered.

"Then you come out here in the hall." His voice was determined.

Bergitta hesitated, then released the latch. "All right, but just for a minute. I have to get my robe."

He reached in and grasped her wrist. "You'll do fine just as you are," he said, pulling her through the door. His eyes ravished the well-proportioned curves revealed through her soft blue gown. She had twisted her hair up and left it there when she washed her face, and the long, graceful neck and cameo profile were displayed to perfection. He stroked the hollow of her throat with his thumb. "You're beautiful," he said simply.

She caught her breath and took a step back. "Have you been drinking?"

"No, but I'm about to," he declared, and for the first time she noticed the bottle of champagne and two stemmed glasses he carried in one hand.

"Not with me, you're not."

He looked around comically. "Then with whom? I don't see anyone else."

"Be serious," she said angrily, her eyes sending storm signals.

He placed the bottle and glasses on a hall table and cupped her face in both his hands. "Oh, but I'm always serious about business, especially when it's unfinished." He lowered his lips and claimed hers. He held her tilted head so tightly that she had no choice but to submit to his advances. If she fought and made a loud noise, her parents would awaken and discover the relationship between her and Jordan was not as they had pretended. She steeled her spine and waited unresponsively for him to finish.

But Jordan was not put off by her stubborn aloofness. His firm but supple lips moved expertly across hers, teasing the corners, then pressing his demands before he once again lightly brushed her lips with featherlight strokes. His sensual advance demanded surrender, but Bergitta refused him the satisfaction, pushing him away when it became apparent he had no intention of withdrawing from where he had pressed her against the wall.

With one hand he captured her wrists and secured them behind her, and with the other he tipped her chin, his eyes sending passionate messages into her own. Bergitta sobbed silently as he kissed away her stubborn refusal and left fiery trails on the slender column of her throat. Unable to control the demands of her own body any longer, she slumped limply against the wall, and that was when he took her in a full embrace, his caresses unchallenged, and even returned with ardor.

"Now perhaps we can have our little toast to the future," he murmured into her hair as he began to finger its lush texture. One by one he removed the pins, allowing the long dark locks to tumble to her shoulders. "Wear it down under your veil tomorrow. It makes you look so innocent when it curves around your face."

"I *am* innocent, Jordan," she said, hoping to bring him to his senses as he began to kiss her eyelids and stroke her cheeks with his thumbs.

"Innocent? Really?" he asked, disbelieving. "You mean the hard-driving executive is inexperienced in love?"

"Jordan," she moaned, "why are you doing this?" With effort she controlled the rampant desires that he

44

was seeking to unleash. His eyes took in her passionate but pained gaze. "I just wanted to make sure this trip was going to be worth the trouble. Now that we understand each other, shall we drink to our honeymoon?"

"You can't do that!" she protested as he was about to pop the cork from the champagne bottle. "You'll wake the entire building." She grabbed his hand, and the bottle plummeted to the floor and crashed into countless pieces.

Mesmerized, they stared at the disaster. Bergitta expected angry reprisals from Jordan, but surprisingly he stood looking at the wasted bottle of liquid as though it had somehow sobered his mood.

He turned to Bergitta. "You go back to bed. I'll take care of this."

Hesitating briefly, Bergitta slipped back into her apartment only to lie awake listening for Jordan's footfall.

Chapter Three

"No, not there. Farther to the right." Bergitta motioned to the stage crew who were placing the festooned wedding bower at the end of the runway. She stuffed her hands in the back pockets of her jeans and studied the effect. "Right there! It's perfect!" She threw a smile to the workers.

Bernie flagged her down just as she was leaving. "You aren't even supposed to be here today," she scolded. "Can't you even take your wedding day off?"

Bergitta grinned. "I slipped in the back door."

Bernie wagged her head. "Jordan assigned Shaw to oversee the final details. He's going to be furious that you stepped into his territory."

The young designer rolled her eyes to the ceiling. "Do you think so?"

Unperturbed she motioned to the florist and showed him where the aisle of tree roses and alternating lamp stands should go. "I'm not too concerned about Shaw's territorial lines," she confided to her assistant. "It's been my experience that if you want something done right, you have to do it yourself!"

"When Jordan couldn't reach you at home, he sent me to find you. He needs you to come to J. W.'s office for a meeting." Seeing Bergitta's raised eyebrows, she said, "He didn't say what the meeting was about."

"He just told you to make sure I got there, right?" she grimaced.

"Right. After that, Libby wants you to try on the sailor number once again, and then Andre´ will be waiting in the salon to do your hair. After that, it's show time!" Bernie announced, making a slitting motion across her neck.

A hard knot rose in Bergitta's throat, and butterflies fluttered in her stomach. In just a few hours, a handful of buyers would decide her future career by the number of orders they turned in. If they liked her designs, her success was assured. If they didn't, not even J. W. could continue to give her the support he had given in the past.

She followed Bernie to J. W.'s office where Jordan was waiting with a man she had never seen before. Jordan was aloof and taciturn. Remembering the two a.m. meeting, Bergitta looked him full in the eye, but his expression was inscrutable.

"Will you excuse us please, Bernie?" he said unsmilingly.

Bernie gave a curt nod and withdrew from the room.

Bergitta perched on a high stool at the office bar and looked from one impassive face to the other. "Is this an occasion I should have dressed for?" she quipped, to excuse her appearance in jeans and T-shirt.

"Bergitta, I'd like you to meet my attorney, Rob Dawson. He has some documents for you to sign. They disclaim any rights to my personal estate in the event of death or injury causing mental incompetence. It's a routine matter."

Stung by his blunt, cold approach, she whipped out, "I wasn't aware you had holdings, Jordan, other than access to your father's estate. Surely you consider him capable of looking after his own interests should anything happen to you."

The attorney cleared his throat nervously at this bit of nastiness and said hastily, "I can assure you Jordan is a man of considerable means. I suggest you read the agreement thoroughly before signing it, and of course, feel free to consult your own attorney if you wish."

He handed her the sheaf of documents. Bergitta felt all the color drain from her face as her eyes fell on the bottom line of the list of holdings. Jordan Wright Worthington III was a wealthy man in his own right without any money from Design House.

Unwittingly, her glance flew to his. She saw from his sardonic smile that he was enjoying the moment! When the color returned to her face, it was in waves of embarrassment.

She held her back erect and walked over to the typewriter at a side desk in the corner, regaining her composure on the way. "I certainly have no problem with this agreement," she said to the attorney, "except that it's incomplete. I'm certain you gentlemen won't mind if I add certain stipulations of my own. I believe that is quite usual in business negotiations."

She sat down and slid the document into the typewriter. Barely suppressing his fury, Jordan stood looking over her shoulder to read her addendum to the marriage contract.

"You can't put that in a public document!" he growled. "This has to be notarized and filed at the courthouse as a matter of public record!"

"Really?" she smiled innocently.

Jordan scowled at the attorney. "Wait in the outer office, Rob. B.G. and I have some talking to do."

Bergitta smiled at his unconscious use of her nickname.

The minute the attorney was out of the room, Jordan wheeled on her. "You must be out of your mind to think you could get by with this. The press would be all over it the second it appeared on record!"

Bergitta lifted her shoulders unconcernedly. "It seems a fair exchange to me. To keep your property rights you give up your connubial rights. You protect the value of your personal worth, and I protect my values, which *are* my personal worth! It seems a fair enough trade."

He ripped the document from the typewriter and tore it in half, his jaw set like iron. Bergitta faced him unflinchingly.

"Of course, there is another kind of agreement we could enter into," she suggested. "It is called mutual trust. I'm not interested in your money, Jordan. I didn't even know you had any. By the same token, you must respect my personhood. Despite the fact that you think I have connived my way to the top, I won't sell myself as part of the bargain!"

"I suppose you felt this was necessary after last night."

"Most certainly."

"I apologize for that."

"Thank you. Apology accepted."

He studied her for several moments. "All right, Bergitta. You have your agreement of mutual trust. You win."

"We both win, Jordan. That's what trust is all about."

André made magic movements with his brush and swirled the curls into smooth waves toward the face.

"It is so supple! It moves like liquid, like brandy!" he exulted in his exaggerated French accent.

Bergitta watched in alarm as he began to put the finishing touches on the hairstyle.

"You're not leaving it that way, are you? I plan to wear it up."

A frown clouded the Frenchman's dark eyes. "But Mr. Worthington specifically sent a request that it was to—"

"Yes, yes I know—" Bergitta sighed impatiently," but it has to be up. All the ad slicks were taken with that style yesterday, remember? We have to be consistent."

"Ah, yes, that is true," he agreed somberly. "But from now on you must dress to please your husband, yes?"

"Of course," she smiled engagingly.

One more interview was waiting when Bergitta reported to the dressing room. After that was done the dressers took her over, the cosmetician getting the first whack at transforming her from designer to bride of the year!

Then she was ready for the dress. The last petal of hand-crocheted lace was patted into place, forming layers of points over the bodice and wider tiers down the skirt. The design was both easy-fitting and feminine. But it also flattered the figure with an innocent sensuality. At ankle length, an underlay of satin cascaded to the floor and trailed into a train edged with the same crocheted lace. Long, tight-fitted sleeves accented slender hands and tapering fingers and a sweetheart neckline provided the perfect frame for the perfect oval face.

The dress had been conceived and created as a work of art and had almost taken on a life of its own. It was a beautiful dress, Brigitta brooded, and it deserved to be worn by a bride who would love it as the bride herself was loved. But such was not the case between Jordan and herself.

Her mother fastened the small wreath of fresh blossoms Bergitta would wear over the forehead. A veil of illusion fell over her face and spilled to a point in back, layering into two veilings.

"Here you go," Bernie whispered, handing her the nosegay attached to a white satin Bible. Bergitta's mother had brought the Bible, which had been used by her great-grandmother and every generation since.

Bergitta caught her breath. Now it was time. It was time to stand before the toughest judges of all—the fickle gods of the industry—the fashion buyers.

She fixed an aloof, mysterious smile on her face just as she had been instructed by the drama coach, waited for his nod of approval, then moved steadily forward, floating, pretending the traditional petal-strewn runway was a cloud and her feet were drifting over it. She had practiced it for hours under the tutelage of the master.

50

By design, she paused and almost seemed to sway backward to add a moment of suspense, and then after everyone had caught the essence of the moment, she picked up the beat and donned a bright eager smile as directed. The luminous candles swathed the bride in a soft halo of light as she glided down the aisle of beribboned tree roses and lampstands.

At the end of the runway she was joined by her father. It was a sentimental moment for him, giving his only daughter in marriage, and for his sake Bergitta wished the circumstances could have been different. The most difficult part of the charade was knowingly deceiving her parents.

Jordan accepted her hand from her father with a crashing look of love that would have fooled even the most skeptical observer. Together they mounted the steps to the wedding bower. Against an improvisational background from a stringed quartet, Jordan and Bergitta were to speak their vows. A spellbound hush settled over the audience as the minister began to speak the words so sacred, so ageless:

"Dearly beloved, we are gathered here today…"

Bergitta stifled a hysterical sob. What was she doing here? What kind of fraud was she participating in? Did this action make her a phony, too? She felt like turning to the audience and screaming out the truth and then running for her life. But where would she run? This *was* her life. It was the one she had chosen for herself—the fast-paced world of always competing to be better than the next.

As though he sensed her distress, Jordan steadied her with his arm. She looked up into his face. It was filled with genuine compassion and was oddly reassuring.

"…For better, for worse, for richer, for poorer, in sickness and in health, to love and to cherish, till death us do part." Bergitta whispered the vows through taut lips, wishing the dastardly act were over. "In token and pledge of our constant faith and abiding love, with this

51

ring, I thee wed…" Bergitta looked down in a daze at the two rings circling her finger.

Then the words of prayer broke into her conscious thoughts like bell tones. "Father, as we join these two together in your sight, may these rings symbolize their relationship to you—two rings representing two filled lives joined at the center by the rock, Christ Jesus, the most pure and timeless gem of all…"

A mist gathered in Bergitta's eyes. How beautiful the ceremony was! And then—

"I now pronounce you husband and wife. The groom may salute his bride."

She felt Jordan's hands lift her veil, felt his hands cup her face, felt his lips claim hers steadily. His fingers caressingly found the way to the pins in her hair which he began to remove gradually one by one. Bergitta stiffened. What was he doing?

Her hair fell to her shoulders, smoothly framing her face as Jordan had said he liked it. Bergitta gasped. There was no mistaking his message. Already he was asserting his authority in this marriage! She was furious.

There was a gentle, crooning ripple through the audience who interpreted the bridegroom's action as a simple, loving intimacy.

"And now," said the minister, "may I present to you Mr. and Mrs. Jordan Wright Worthington III."

Bells chimed out from the bell choir as Jordan helped Bergitta slowly turn to greet the company.

The trumpets heralded, and the bride and groom began the stately processional back up the runway, Bergitta doing her best to look appropriately happy. The trumpets added the final note of grandeur to the occasion, but it was the thunderous applause that was music to Bergitta's ears. She had done it! The show was a success!

Later, as Bergitta slid into the green suit with the slashed skirt and neckline that had been designed for Clare, she was grateful to be excused from the wine party where the buyers were busily filling out orders. The models would circulate among the buyers, allowing them to feel the fabrics and study the detail of a costume at close range. Since the bridal gown was an original, it could not be ordered, although undoubtedly close copies would be made of the unique design.

"Mother, would you hand me the shoes?" She balanced herself with one hand on her mother's shoulders while she fastened the dainty straps of the opera pumps. "Bernie will give you a copy of my itinerary for the next two months."

"She already has, dear. You seem to be rushing about mighty fast."

"Can't be helped, Mother. We have to get the shots done in time for the next two issues of the magazines we contracted with for coverage."

"My goodness! You make it sound as though this marriage were concocted for the convenience of publicity!"

"Does it sound that way, Mother? I'm sorry. It just seemed an ideal way to honeymoon without losing the momentum of interest in the styles. Just think! I'll be on the company yacht, the *Ocean Queen*. You can look for me in all the fashionable spots of the world—London in front of Big Ben and Buckingham Palace, Amsterdam for the tulip festival, the ruins of Rome, and then on to Paris where we'll visit fashion houses. Doesn't that sound exciting?" She patted her mother's face as though the older woman were the child who had to be placated.

"Humph!" growled her father. "I'd a lot rather see you behind the cookpots on a kitchen stove where women belong."

"Now, Dad," Bergitta grinned, wagging a playful finger at him. "I promise you that's an argument you won't win around here."

André came to brush in a style now that her hair was down, casting her a knowing wink; Libby checked her hemline and accessories, and Bernie stood by to announce Jordan's arrival.

Bergitta discovered her parents on the verge of tears. "Hey, you two! Stop that crying," she smiled at her misty-eyed mother. "We can visit any time we want by phone."

"But things will never be the same again, dear."

"They never are, Mother," Bergitta said solemnly, for suddenly it became clear to her, too, that she was closing this phase of her life forever. Even after an annulment, she would never be Bergitta Blakely again. She would be the ex-Mrs. Worthington, and everyone would always wonder what had gone wrong and who was at fault.

Amidst flying particles of rice and camera flashes, Bergitta was hurried to the waiting limousine by an ostensibly eager bridegroom to begin their "new life" together. Although she had dreaded setting out on this voyage with Jordan, she was so weary of the media interviews and photograph sessions that she now looked forward to some quiet time alone in a cozy cabin. There would be three days of nothing but sun and sea. How delicious!

At dockside they were met by the captain of the ninety-foot yacht. He handed his guest of honor a bouquet of yellow roses, and once again there was the inescapable photographer asking her to pose for more pictures. This time it was the photographer who would be traveling with them, the one who did Clare's assignments.

She was introduced to the tall, thin, sandy-haired man named Christopher Jamison. He acknowledged her with a furtive smile, which she did not understand any more than she understood Jordan's veiled hostility toward him.

Chris, as he was called, stroked his thin blond mustache as he tried to choose the best location for a silhouette shot of the newlyweds against the sunset. "Over by the railing, I think, hovering together just before a kiss—no, no!" he interrupted himself. "Let's go ahead and have the kiss, but instead of leaning against the deck rail, let's try it over by the ship's wheel."

Jordan blew out his breath in exasperation and uttered an oath. "Can't you see we're worn out? Have a little consideration! You'll get your pictures, but not until Bergitta and I have had a couple of days' rest!"

Chris made no attempt to hide his anger. "I was assured I would have your full cooperation on this cruise," he sneered.

For an answer, Jordan tucked Bergitta's arm into his and led the way to their quarters.

She was surprised at how ample their accommodations were. A sitting room in varying shades of blue was accented in white and black. There were a wet bar, hot plate, and refrigerator in one alcove, and a sleeper sofa in another. Stereo music played as the lights went up. There was a spacious bath with a spa tub, and the bedroom had the ultimate in a waterbed and a magnificent view of the ocean through sliding glass doors leading to the deck. The blue shades were soft and restful pastels, from the satin sheets on the bed to the velvety towels in the bathroom.

"Nice," Bergitta commented approvingly. She was too tired to bring up how their sleeping quarters were to be divided and decided she would soak in a luxurious bubble bath up to her neck before she tackled anything that was going to require any energy.

Minutes later she was afloat in a sea of bubbles, her mind drifting off as free as a seagull gliding on the wind. The weeks of hard work getting ready for the show and the days of emotional tension brought on by the sudden wedding dropped from her into nothingness. She knew that already her labors had been fruitful. Bernie had whispered in her ear just as she was getting into the limo that buyers were turning in orders in quantities surpassing all prognostications. As soon as the trip had accomplished its advertising and public-relation purposes, Bergitta Blakely would be as renowned as the famous Chanel. Perhaps she, too, would have her own brand of perfume, Bergitta dreamed away.

"Dive under! I'm coming in!" Jordan boomed as he burst robustly through the door. He bent low over the sink and turned both faucets on full force.

Bergitta slid under the blanket of bubbles all the way to her chin, startled by his forceful entrance.

"Thunder!" Jordan fumed as he scrambled for a bottle of pills in the medicine cabinet and, finding them, tossed two down with a paper cup of water. "I always get seasick the first few hours out to sea," he explained with a little boy's abashment. "I'll be better now."

Bergitta screamed with laughter. "Jordan! We haven't even left port yet!"

"Don't laugh!" he warned. "You don't know what your own reactions will be when we get into deep water."

Bergitta gulped. "I've never sailed before. How bad is it?"

"It can be very serious," Jordan said soberly.

"Really?" Bergitta paled.

"We lose one or two at sea every voyage," he said with the corner of his mouth twitching mischievously.

"Oh, Jordan. Get out of here!" Bergitta hissed, realizing he was making sport of her.

The laughter in his eyes faded into a warmth that wrapped her in his gaze.

Bergitta shrank further into the suds. "I see you are not too sick to stand there and ogle me!"

Jordan laughed at her expression, then said, "I'd have to be sick indeed not to appreciate a beautiful woman." He closed the bathroom door and leaned against it, arms folded over his chest. "Most women like to be appreciated," he pointed out, grinning.

Bergitta's eyes widened. It appeared that he wasn't

planning to leave, and she suddenly remembered last night's escapade with the champagne bottle.

"Are you planning to leave or not, Jordan?" The icicles in her warning voice were a strong barometer for what his answer should be.

"Only if you promise to give up the bathroom soon. The ship's crew is planning a wedding dinner for us at eight, and word has filtered down that there is to be a 'surprise' *bon voyage* party," he grimaced. "It seems everyone wants to help us celebrate our marriage and the success of the show."

Bergitta groaned. "I'm exhausted, Jordan. I can handle dinner, but not a party that's likely to go on until all hours of the morning."

"My sentiments exactly," he agreed. "Well, I know how to handle this. We'll plan a surprise for them, instead."

There was a decisive determination about him when he left, and Bergitta understood his innuendo when a few minutes later she felt the yacht rock as the engines turned. There was a sliding, lifting motion. Apparently the captain had gotten his orders, and they were underway, leaving behind any *bon voyage* party plans.

At dinner, Bergitta met the members of the crew, which totaled only five besides Captain Stu. Libby was traveling with them to attend to wardrobe needs. Since the whole purpose of the trip was to "frame" the clothes in an international setting, every thread must be perfect. The cabin steward and the cook were a lovely couple who had retired from the sea and had taken the job aboard the company-owned yacht for its occasional voyages. They were Mac and Myrtice. Both had wide smiles and jovial personalities that conveyed they enjoyed every moment of life. Libby seemed to hit it off with Myrtice right away, their congenial personalities honing in on each other. The engineer and first mate made a brief appearance, then went below to take care of some technicality with the ship's computer system.

The food was excellent. Roast duckling cooked to a crispy turn and lavished with purple plum sauce was accompanied by tips of asparagus sautéed with fresh mushrooms and a blend of spices. A chocolate soufflé was served for dessert with cups of café Vienna. Chris and Libby's conversation naturally turned to the afternoon's design show, but Bergitta found herself curiously disinterested. She was suffering a case of burnout, and her attention wandered to Myrtice who was showing Jordan pictures from her Grandma's Brag Book album. He pretended avid interest in the two-year-old, but fidgeted impatiently and finally caught Bergitta's eye over Myrtice's head. He signaled that he was ready to excuse them from the dinner party so they could return to their cabin suite.

Quickly stalling, Bergitta asked Myrtice, "How many more children do you have besides the mother of your two grandsons?"

Thirty minutes later they had seen the last picture, and Jordan rose to his feet. "I'm sure no one here will be offended if we adjourn this company early tonight, so if you will excuse us, Bergitta and I will plan on seeing you all sometime before we reach England." He winked broadly and joined in the laughter, pulling back her chair before Bergitta could devise some other way to delay their departure.

While Jordan sorted out the luggage, Bergitta went into the bathroom and changed from her dinner dress into a simple white silk, crepe lounging pajama embroidered with gold scrolls below the gathers of the dropped shoulders. It was part of the trousseau planned for Clare, and since it was not one of the items to be photographed, Bergitta had not concerned herself with having alterations made for her more generous figure. But she luxuriated in the softness of the fabric.

Jordan raised his eyebrows in surprise. "If you expect me to keep my end of the agreement, the least you could do is make it easy for me. Put some cold cream on your face or something."

"It's not my face that's bothering you," she pointed out dryly. "Sorry. I didn't bring any sackcloth and ashes."

"The way I feel now, you would look good to me even in that."

"Deal with it, Jordan," she said coldly, picking up a book.

He accepted her rejection as a challenge. "I know I could change your mind." He came near her and lifted a curl from her ear with a lightly massaging forefinger.

She took a quick breath as she felt her body shock from his sensuous touch. "No doubt you could. My hormones are perfectly normal. On the other hand, so are my other appetites. One could get accustomed to living in luxury such as this," she motioned about her. "If a divorce became necessary instead of an annulment, not even your attorney would expect me to waive a settlement."

Her words had the effect of a cold shower. "You really are just what I supposed you to be, aren't you?" he sneered. "You would stop at nothing to get what you want! Has it ever occurred to you that should you pull a trick like that you would be finished at Design House since I am now the chief?"

"And has it occurred to you that it really wouldn't matter since I now could go with any design firm I choose and probably name my own price at that?"

They squared off on even ground.

"You are tough, Mrs. Worthington."

"Don't call me Mrs. Worthington."

"Why not? Like it or not, that is who you are."

"I am not. I am Bergitta Blakely, designer."

"If that is all you are, Bergitta, your life must be sadly one-sided. Is there never room for another human being in your life? We have two months to spend together, Bergitta. It would be much easier to make love than to fight." He pulled her to him and embrassed her possessively. As she was about to cry out, his lips closed over hers and his warm breath intoxicated her.

"I've never wanted a wife before," he murmured in a softly sensuous voice, continuing his persuasion with lips that randomly explored the sensitive areas so vulnerable to his touch. Against her will she responded to his passion. *Why not?* She thought wildly. *We are legally married.* She clung to him and pressed against his hard chest, thrilling to the touch of her body against his. When he moved toward the bed, she went helplessly with him, no longer trying to justify her own desires.

He felt for the fastener at the back of her pajamas, and the reality of his intentions caused her suddenly to twist free. "We have an agreement, Jordan. Can't you see how this could complicate matters?"

His answer was interrupted by the strident ring of the ship-to-shore telephone. Jordan impatiently snatched up the phone, and Bergitta seized the opportunity to slide into some jeans and a sweater.

"Hello!" Jordan fairly snarled into the phone. "Oh, it's you, Clare." His voice softened. Bergitta wheeled in time to see a soft transformation in his face.

She whirled and fled from the room. To think she had almost let him persuade her into bed with him, she fumed. The sliding door to the deck closed quietly behind her, and she disappeared into the fog that had gathered since nightfall. She paced around the deck a time or two, not expecting to see anyone since everyone else on board was quartered below. She needed the sharp spring air to clear her mind.

It was obvious that whatever were Clare and Jordan's problems, they had resolved them. No doubt the call last evening during dinner at Jordan's home was an attempt to stop the wedding. Judging from the friendly attitude Jordan had greeted her with just now, he was wishing her here. How unfortunate that this state of affairs couldn't have been achieved *before* the engagement between Jordan and herself was announced, Bergitta thought bitterly. She wouldn't have had to waste six months of her life married to Jordan! And how sure Clare must be of Jordan, to call him on his wedding night! She wondered what Clare would have thought had she known she had just interrupted seduction on the high seas perpetrated by her unfaithful lover! Bergitta laughed mirthlessly and stared into the dark swirling water below.

The hollow sound of footsteps penetrated the fog, and she could barely make out the light of a cigarette. The bare outline of a trench coat became visible, and then Bergitta recognized Chris. He pretended surprise, but she had the feeling he had been watching her all the time. She shivered as he placed his hand on her arm.

"What is this?" he asked mockingly. "Isn't it usually the groom who goes for the stroll to allow the blushing, bashful bride time to collect her nerve?"

He grated on her nerves. She muttered through gritted teeth, "What are you doing here? This part of the deck is private."

His steely blue eyes cut her like a knife. "It didn't take you long to adopt the Worthington authority once you became part of the family hierarchy, did it?"

Bergitta ignored the implication and turned on her heel. Chris fell into step with her. "Aren't you going back to your cabin?"

"When I accomplish what I came to do."

"What did you come to do, Mrs. Worthington?"

"I came out here to spend some time alone," she said pointedly. "What did *you* come here to do?"

"The same thing. It's crowded downstairs, and I didn't anticipate your making an appearance before dawn."

They walked in silence. A breeze blew up, and in a matter of minutes the fog had dissipated, unveiling a blue evening sky washed golden from the rising moon.

"Jordan should be here with you. Why isn't he?"

Bergitta disliked his nosy attitude and was insulted by his presumptuous familiarity.

"I think I'll go in now," she announced, having decided she wasn't going to be able to shake the photographer.

"I'll walk with you to the cabin."

"It isn't necessary. I'm sure I'll be safe enough."

He walked with her anyway, and she was chagrined when he commented that he would like to spend some time getting to know her. He said he always photographed his subjects better after he understood their personalities.

They were at the door. Unexpectedly he said, "I never did get my turn to kiss the bride today. Do you mind?"

Before she could voice her objections, he leaned over, his lips poised over her mouth, when a stream of light poured over them. Jordan stood in the open doorway, scowling.

"I see you two have taken advantage of a moonlit evening."

"Don't be a fool, Worthington," Chris rasped. "You know I always take every opportunity to study my photographic subjects."

"Let's just say you take every opportunity!" Jordan growled, his face contorted with fury.

"Excuse me." Bergitta eased around Jordan to enter the cabin. She was amazed at the hostility between the two men. Obviously something was wrong between Clare's fiancé and her photographer. But what?

Chapter Four

The next morning Bergitta awoke on the sofa where she had fallen asleep reading the latest best seller, for which she finally had time. The churning and pitching in her stomach told her immediately that she had fallen victim to the malady of the sea. She bolted through the bedroom on her way to the bathroom.

Without a word Jordan got some ice from the refrigerator in the bar alcove, wrapped it in a wet bath cloth, and held it to her forehead. With the other hand he foraged in the medicine cabinet for the bottle of pills and held the cup while she gulped them down.

"I...I don't think I can make it back to the sofa," she said weakly.

He lifted her and carried her to the bed, staying to bathe her face with the cold cloth. He felt her pulse and told her to say "ahhh." She stuck her tongue out at him. He laughed from deep within and told Bergitta that his diagnosis assured him she would live. She noticed, however, that his scrutiny of her condition was serious.

"Do I look as green as I feel?" she smiled wanly.

He pretended to do an in-depth inspection before he answered. "You'd be a good match for the green gown you wore to the gala," he affirmed.

She groaned. "Is it that bad?"

"From the looks of it, you're in for a bad seige. I'm

going to put a pitcher of water beside the bed. Take a sip every few minutes."

"Yuk," was Bergitta's answer.

"I know it tends to make you sick again, but drink it anyway. You have to keep fluids in your body."

He spoke with easy authority, and Bergitta had the impression he was knowledgeable.

"I feel dizzy and drowsy."

"It's the pills. They have that effect. Close your eyes, and I'll take the pillow from under your head. That should help."

She was in and out of a drugged sleep, and each time she woke to give in once again to the horrible wretchings, he was there, insisting she take sips of water. When she refused, he gave her crushed ice from a spoon.

The next day was worse. There was a storm, and the swells rose ten feet high. "I'd rather be dead," Bergitta moaned. Jordan made no response except to insist that she drink some of the broth he had asked Myrtice to bring in.

She pushed the cup away. "I can't."

Grimly, he said, "You don't have a choice, Bergitta. Either you drink the fluids and eat the Jell-O, or I'm going to radio the Coast Guard to get a hospital helicopter here. You are dangerously dehydrated."

Her head whirled deliriously. "How do you know that?"

He hesitated, then answered in simple but decisive terms. "Trust me. I know."

She obediently took the Jell-O from the tip of the spoon he offered. The bite was so small she was able to keep it down without her stomach's objecting. Every five minutes he fed her another infinitesimal bite.

For three days he was monitoring her condition, never far from her side.

By the third day she was improved enough to walk a few minutes on deck and take light solids. The next day when she awoke feeling weak but fresh for the first time, Jordan applauded her. "You are hereby declared an old sea salt," he grinned.

For the first time in days food smelled good to her. On the way down to breakfast, dressed in cut-off jeans and a red-striped tee shirt, she cast puzzled glances at Jordan. He caught her in the act as they took the stairs down to the dining room.

"What is it, Bergitta? You seem to have a question," he smiled.

His smile was warm and inviting, the straight even teeth sparkling from its vivacity.

Thoughtful, she said, "You knew just what to do, didn't you?"

"About your seasickness you mean? Of course. I've encountered it several times."

"No, it was more than being familiar with what to do Dehydration isn't easily recognized. It takes an expert to diagnose it."

"Well, maybe I've had experience," he brushed her query away.

Everyone in the dining room cheered when Bergitta walked in. She grinned and saluted, announcing that she was starved.

Myrtice brought a platter of delicate cheese omelets and a smaller side platter of tiny pink sausages, ham, and crisp bacon. There were crisp potato pancakes and cushiony biscuits with creamy butter.

Jordan watched Bergitta sail into the food with zest. After her third potato pancake, he burst into laughter. "This wife of mine is trying for the Miss Piggy award!"

Bergitta grinned back, somewhat abashed by his attention, but not enough to surrender her fork and plate.

After breakfast the entire company gathered on the deck with steaming cups of coffee. The sea was peaceful, and the sun was already warm on their bare legs. Mac began stories of his years at sea and the ports of the world he had seen. Most often the stories were embellished and finally finished by Myrtice who had a flair for dramatizing the simplest event.

In such good company Bergitta opened up like a bud to the sun. Several times she discovered Jordan's eyes following her after she had contributed her own comical story or animatedly shared a joke. She enjoyed the lighthearted banter with Mac and teased him about his balding forehead.

He stroked his thick beard and answered in his hometown drawl, "Wal, we grow it whar we kin."

Jordan seemed to be giving scant attention to the nonsensical chatter, but he gave full attention to Bergitta, his interest keen on her every move.

"Time to rest," he said after an hour on deck. "You don't want to overdo it on your first day up." He gave her his hand.

Reluctantly she followed him and rested on the sofa in the cool sitting room while he made some ship-to-shore phone calls. His conversations were terse and to the point, having to do mostly with buying or selling stocks and pieces of real estate. When he was finished he announced his intention to go diving.

"*What?*" Bergitta squeaked. "Way out here in the middle of the ocean?"

"The navigational charts note a rock formation that I want to explore. Who knows? I may even find an old ship lodged there and bring up a treasure chest full of rubies and diamonds," he chuckled playfully.

Bergitta was riddled with fear. "All the experts say it's dangerous to dive without a companion."

"Are you volunteering?"

If anything horrified her more than Jordan's diving into the fathoms of the deep, it was the idea of *her* going scuba diving.

"Absolutely not." She shook her head adamantly. "But someone should."

"Stu is going." Jordan set her fears at rest. "He and I

66

usually have a go at it when we're on one of these excursions."

Excitement mounted on his face and in his body as he paced back and forth on the deck, checking his air tank and adjusting his gear. Stu was there, eager also, but his impatience was nothing like Jordan's whose eyes were lit with a driving fire.

Clutching the rail so tightly her fingers grew numb, Bergitta watched them submerge. "Is it safe for the captain to be away from the boat?" she squeaked nervously.

"He wouldn't have it any other way," the first mate informed her. "Jordan is too adventuresome, and Stu goes to make sure he doesn't go too far or take unnecessary risks."

"Jordan does that?"

"All the time and at everything he does," the first mate affirmed, and Bergitta saw that he wasn't kidding.

Libby and Bergitta watched for the two to surface. There was a break in the water, and Stu cleared his mask and yelled back for a rope. Bergitta clutched Libby's arm. Where was Jordan?

Seeing her anxiety, Mac joined them. "Don't worry. It wasn't a distress signal. If it had been, you can be sure we would be reeling up the life line by now."

"Then why would they need a rope?" Libby asked.

"They may have found something they want to bring up."

Just then Jordan and Stu surfaced. They climbed the ladder and rejoined the crew with smiles as big as the ship's broadside.

"We found something!" Jordan announced. "It appears to be a section of a hospital ship, maybe from World War II. The water was surprisingly clear, and the Red Cross insignia was still visible. There's an air pocket in the section, and that means there's a good chance of finding identifiable material."

"You're not going to try to bring it up, are you?" Mac

asked, obviously disapproving.

"Of course!" Jordan said, his eyes gleaming.

Stu and his first mate exchanged glances. "That's a life-threatening situation down there," Stu challenged him. "The openings through the rock formations are narrow and as sharp as knives. I'd be afraid of a severe injury."

"Then you'd better not go with me," Jordan said cryptically.

"No," Stu shot out, "maybe neither of us should go!" He stalked off, and the others dispersed, uncomfortable over the abrupt exchange.

Later in the cabin Bergitta turned on Jordan. "Are you crazy? Have you forgotten we're on a working tour? If you were severely injured the whole ad campaign would be shot to pieces!"

"Your concern for my welfare is touching," Jordan smiled caustically. "However, there's really no reason for alarm. Stu is overstating the problem. There is a circular rock formation with a bowl-shaped opening in the center. Tomorrow I'll go in the same way the ship did—over the top of the rocks and down into the cavern."

His excitement had reached mammoth proportions again. It was plain he was beyond reason.

"What drives you, Jordan? Why must you do this?" Bergitta had picked up her manicure set and had begun filing her nails out of sheer nervous energy. He was pacing the sitting room, on fire with his plans.

"Why do it?" he shouted incredulously. "I should think that would be obvious. Don't you have any spirit of adventure? Do you realize how often a diver comes across a find that is within his reach? Almost never! The fact that it is part of the remains of a hospital ship is doubly important to me."

"Why?"

Suddenly he fell silent. There was a long pause before he finally shrugged and said, "It just is. I happen to have an interest in the medical profession."

The next day Bergitta watched as Jordan lowered himself over the side. Stu followed, having negotiated a compromise with Jordan to use hooks on the ends of long poles to try to dislodge the materials and let them float to the top. Jordan had argued that the find might sink farther to the bottom, but agreed to experiment with Stu's procedure.

Stu was grim when he followed Jordan, and Bergitta realized the whole matter had ceased to be a lark. Jordan's determination had pressed the crew's patience.

Mac stood by, ready to lower one of the lifeboats to row out and pick up any debris that might float up to the surface. Fifteen minutes passed and nothing happened. The sea was glassy bright, and those on board were a somber company waiting for the divers to reappear.

"I'm going on down," Mac growled, cutting loose one of the life boats. They only have a few minutes' more air in their tanks."

"Don't take any chances," Myrtice said quickly.

"I won't," he promised, buckling on a life jacket.

He had just begun to row when Stu broke the surface. "He cut his rope loose!" Stu yelled. "We couldn't reach it, and he has gone into the pit alone!"

Bergitta went nauseous. She had no way of knowing how experienced a diver Jordan was, but she could almost smell danger. Judging from the pasty faces of her companions, she had sized up the situation accurately. The tension was thick as the minutes ticked off without a sign of the daring diver. It seemed like an eternity before a shout of victory split the morning.

"*Ya hoo!*" Jordan's shout reverberated over the deep. "I've got it!" He waved the boat toward him, treading water with one hand and lugging a bobbing object with the other. Stu and Mac picked Jordan out of the water and hauled in a shapeless black object. They spent the next half hour retrieving other debris that was floating to the surface, mostly wood and odd bits of metal.

Chris was busily changing lenses on his camera to take shots of the excursion with his telescope attachment. There was no small excitement when Jordan climbed over the side of the ship with his prize—a black leather bag belonging to a doctor whose name was engraved in gold letters on the side. He grabbed Bergitta in a victory hug, and while she appreciated his exuberance, she was still miffed at the chance he had taken. Sensing this, he invited her to be the first to open the bag. Together they bent over it.

"How could it be in such perfect condition?" she asked, feeling the smooth-grained leather which bore no signs of deterioration from water or salt.

"It was trapped in an air space. Leather is practically indestructible anyway. It was lodged on top of a pile of other furniture in a crevice that somehow escaped water. Strange, isn't it?"

Bergitta examined the gold letters done in old English script. "Walter C. Halstrom, M. D.," she read in awe.

Reverently, Jordan ran his hand over the black case. "He paid his full dues."

Opening the case proved to be no simple matter. Lubricants and pliers were required to inch the zipper open tooth by tooth. While the brass was not rusted, it was welded together by the passage of time.

When at last they were able to pry the opening apart, Jordan took out the instruments, handling them almost with familiarity, it seemed to Bergitta. There was no damage to the instruments—a stethoscope, some thermometers, and various other tools of the trade. Inside, Dr. Halstrom's address was inked on an identification card still held in a pocket.

Bergitta and Jordan had the same thought and voiced it as their glances met. The Halstrom family should have this back, if they could be found. During their stay in London they could try to locate the Brighton address.

70

Stu and Mac had their chance to look through the contents of the physician's bag. Mac held up a half-full bottle of brandy.

"I'm sure this was a necessary part of the good doctor's portable dispensary," he chuckled. "Come on, Jordan. Open it and have a belt—a last toast to Dr. Halstrom, whoever he may be."

Jordan took the bottle and turned it over in his palm. Soberly he said, "Perhaps it would be more of a toast to the doctor's good works if I abstained."

With that, Jordan replaced the contents of the bag and carried it to the cabin. Bergitta followed and puzzled over his response to Mac's suggestion.

Jordan stripped out of his wet suit, but left on his swimwear. He suggested she join him on their private deck for a sunning session.

Lying beside him on a towel, Bergitta observed him closely. He had practically challenged death and was the winner. Now he seemed totally at peace with himself and so blissfully happy that he might almost have been in a hypnotic state.

As though knowing she was watching him, he turned over and propped on one elbow to return her observation. He reached out a forefinger and traced the delicate curve of her oval face.

"How did you get that incredible tan so early in the season?" He smiled lazily.

"I believe in sun lamps year round," she smiled back. She had put a short triangular white eyelet scarf over her hair to protect it from the rays. The matching swimsuit contrasted beautifully with her smooth tan.

"Mmmm." His eyes traveled over her tan. "You look good enough to eat." He leaned over and nibbled playfully at her ear, declaring it the cutest he had ever seen.

She raised her eyebrows in amusement. "Cute ears? You'll have to do better than that."

Taking her challenge as an invitation, he cautiously tantalized her eyelids and teased her pink cheeks with

71

his lips. It was all she could do to keep from curling her arms around his neck and pulling him down to her. When she could manage to control her breath, she sat up. "Come on, let's go to the dining room. Isn't it time for lunch?"

He laughed at her obvious attempt to distract his interest. "You're foiled again. Myrtice is bringing up a sandwich tray."

Nevertheless, Bergitta slipped into a coverup and leaned against the leg of a deck chair, drawing her knees up under her chin. "What is it like so far down in the ocean?" she asked with curiosity.

He reached out and absentmindedly began tickling her toes. "Oh...it's like nothing you have ever seen before," he said dreamily. "The quiet is indescribable. The beauty is unsurpassed. There is a sense of complete serenity like a symphony that has just completed the perfect overture. The order of life down there is perfectly synchronized."

"You sound just like a poet."

"I cannot imagine trying to describe it in any other way." His eyes beckoned her from soft lazy depths. "Come over here, Bergitta. I want to tell you something."

Surprised into acquiescence, she went to sit beside him on the towel. "What is it, Jordan?"

"This." He gathered her into his arms and kissed her deeply, quelling her impulse to resist. She felt his arms claiming her and drawing her firmly to his body. Her arms circled his back, feeling the strong ripples of his muscles flex under the pressure of her caressing hands.

His torrid kisses inflamed her, and the heated flare of his passions compelled her to accompany him into yet another venture as exciting and dangerous as the heady depths of the sea. She wanted him to kiss her forever, to hold her until only eternity would release her from his love spell. The rough texture of his clean-shaven jaw and the roughened voice that repeated her name passionately held her.

"Jordan, Jordan," she whispered on the wings of breathless gasps, "hold me, love me!" She cried out in rapture.

The familiar sound of whirring clicks brought them both upright to see Chris taking shots with his camera. Jordan covered the distance in a flash and with one powerful swing knocked the camera out of his hands.

"Swine!" Chris squalled, animal-like. He clenched his fist and was halfway into a swing when Jordan's grip closed on his forearm in mid air. "I wouldn't try that if I were you," he said menacingly. "Even a photographer should learn that some things are private."

Jordan reached down and picked up the camera, releasing the lock and freeing the film.

Furious almost beyond control, Chris spat, "What's your problem, Jordan? Are you afraid the prints might fall into the wrong hands? Destroy all the film you like. I have a very descriptive picture in my mind that Clare might be very interested in."

"I doubt Clare would listen to *anything* you have to say, Jamison." He took two or three steps toward him. "Now clear out!"

Bergitta pressed the clenched knuckles of both hands to her teeth, biting hard on them to stop the cries of anguish that rose in her throat. Even Chris knew it was not over between Clare and Jordan. What a fool he must think her! And Jordan had used her.

She turned and fled into the shower to scrub off the suntan oil and her shame. Jordan came in and called to her through the shower curtain.

"Bergitta, it's not what you think. I want to explain."

"Go away. There's nothing to explain. You and Chris have just made everything abundantly clear."

"I'm not leaving until you listen. And I don't think you want to walk out of there without your towel." He snatched it from the overhead rod away from her reach.

"You perverted—"

"Watch it! You're a lady," he reminded her with laughter in his voice.

"I'm surprised you noticed! You certainly haven't treated me like one."

"I didn't notice any unwillingness on your part out there just now, Bergitta," he said provokingly.

There was silence for a moment, and then she mumbled, "You do things to me, Jordan."

"I know. I love it," he chuckled. Then he continued seriously, "There's nothing wrong with what was between us—" he began, but Bergitta interrupted him.

"There is *everything* wrong with this charade, Jordan. It's dishonest to ourselves and to others. I just want to get through this as gracefully as I can, and then you and Clare can go on with your plans. It's too bad you didn't settle your differences before the show instead of afterwards."

There was total silence, and Bergitta had begun to wonder if he was still there.

"You don't know what you're talking about, Bergitta. There is absolutely nothing between Clare and me. In fact, what I've come to realize is that there never was."

"If what you say is true, why does she continue to call you?"

He heaved a sigh. "Clare has problems Bergitta—serious problems that I'm not free to discuss."

"I see," Bergitta said coldly.

"Believe me, Bergitta," Jordan said humbly. "I would like nothing better than to explain the circumstances, but I can't. I can only ask you to trust me so that we can become friends."

"It seems to me you want more than friendship, Jordan, and I'm not prepared to go the distance." She reached a hand out for the towel, and he gave it to her. She stepped out of the shower with the towel tightly knotted around her. Her long shapely legs extended below the short blue towel, making her more desirable than ever.

She picked up a brush and blow dryer and began to pull the brush through her thick wet hair. "Despite what you think about my career fixation, some day I hope to find myself in love and being loved by a very special person whom I will love for who he is. Then, a physical relationship will mean something. Until that happens, I want no substitute relationship, even with someone I happen to be legally married to for the sake of a convenient business necessity. Marriage happens in the heart, not in the board room."

"If that's really how you want it, I can accept that," Jordan nodded. "Even if we can't be lovers, let's not be enemies." He offered his hand and she placed hers in his tight grasp.

"Friends?" he smiled.

"Friends!" she agreed, smiling at him gratefully.

Chapter Five

"I'm not going to make an idiot of myself by mimicking a clock!" Bergitta hissed, hoping to avoid making a scene in front of the amused passersby. "Besides, this black outfit is much too sophisticated for flailing arms and an imitation of Big Ben!" Forgetting to keep her pitch low, she was now storming wrathfully at the insistent photographer.

"It's not your job to script the shots," Chris bit out. "Cut out the temperamental floor show, and let's get on with it." Visibly calming his own anger, he said, "Point the right arm straight up to twelve and the left arm to three. Cross your ankles."

"I can't keep that pose for more than a second," she objected.

The photographer shrugged his shoulders. "So, if you tip over backwards, you'll just have to do it over again," he said indifferently.

Bergitta sighed and flexed her tired muscles before getting into position again for the hundredth pose that day. She adjusted the fedora one more time, and stood still while Libby tugged at the material gathered under the belt of the double-breasted silk coat. Sheer black stockings and black patent pumps gave the outfit a very chic look. They were shooting for an ad segment entitled, "Timely Evening Fashions for the Bride."

It was three a.m. in London. Chris had insisted on shooting at exactly this time so his shots of Big Ben in the background would be authentic. The evening was wet and cold, and, to the photographer's delight, fog was rolling in. He said it would add that much more atmosphere to the shot. Bergitta was chilled to the bone, and every muscle ached.

"Let's get on with it," an irritated Chris persisted.

Like an automaton she stood on the marked spot and raised her right arm straight up while pointing her left arm out in the three o'clock position.

"No, I said the opposite. Left arm up, right arm out."

"You didn't."

"Yes I did."

Jordan, who had accompanied them on the photographic expedition, interrupted, "Does it matter?"

"Not unless you're the one standing up here," Bergitta said with saccharin sweetness.

"Take it like a dose of medicine," Jordan suggested. "Get it over with as fast as possible."

One more time Bergitta went into the pose, determinedly promising herself it was the last time. Three poses later Chris finally released her, and they went back to the Ritz Carlton Hotel. Bergitta limped into the lobby, half walking and half carried by Jordan.

He inserted the key in the lock, and in that moment she slumped against him, sound asleep. He lifted her and carried her inside, then shook her gently. Dazed, she began to weep uncontrollably.

Jordan tucked her head under his chin and stroked her hair just as he might console a child.

"There's no sense in Chris's driving so hard," she sniffed. "One hundred shots of the same scene is totally out of reason."

"I'm sure it seems so," Jordan said soothingly. "But remember, he's the best. He knows what he's doing. That's the only reason I put up with him after—" A note of disgust had crept into his voice, but it was quickly replaced by mischief. "Tomorrow you'll feel different. Would you allow a good friend to help you get undressed for bed?" he grinned.

She gulped and nodded. "I'm too tired to resist."

"That's a dangerous thing to admit. A fellow could take advantage."

"I wouldn't try," she bristled, suddenly wide awake.

She sat on the bed while he eased off her slippers, took off her fedora, and removed her jewelry. She felt her head droop as she slipped blissfully into black oblivion.

When she awoke the next morning, she found herself clad only in her undies and her blue satin robe.

"It was done with the greatest finesse," he assured her as he saw her blush with embarrassment. "Your modesty is preserved. I turned my head as a gentleman should."

Bergitta stared at him in disbelief. "I suppose you have undressed so many women that by now it means nothing to you," she babbled to cover her humiliation.

"A few," he agreed, "but I wouldn't go so far as to say it means nothing to me!" A quirk appeared at the corner of his mouth and his eyes gleamed with laughter.

She sailed a pillow across the room. He dodged expertly and flung it back at her. "Now, if you will behave I will serve you coffee in bed. You deserve it after all your hard work last night."

She sipped the luscious hot liquid and asked, "What time is it?"

"Noon. Are you hungry?"

"Not very. I'm still too tired to eat."

"Are you too tired to take one of the tour buses around London?"

"No. I'd love that," she beamed at him.

The last few days Jordan had been heavenly. He had been the kind, considerate person that she had not known he could be. Apparently he had taken seriously her petition to establish a platonic relationship.

Watching him as he moved about the room, she wondered if she had really been in her right mind. He was the most handsome and virile man she had ever met. His shoulder muscles swelled under the knit shirt he was wearing, and his proud bearing and strong profile were a source of joy. Her eyes traveled the length of him, from his well-set head to the narrow, tapered hips and sturdy legs. She closed her eyes and allowed herself the luxury of remembering how it had felt to be held by him, to have his body pressing to her own until it seemed they would meld together, never to separate.

"Up with you," he flung the pale blue, satin coverlet aside and swung her legs to the gray-carpeted floor. "Wear something comfortable."

She took him at his word and threw on an old pair of jeans dignified only by a white, long-sleeved sweat shirt which she chose to belt with a wide, leather cummerbund.

"You look beautiful in anything," he declared admiringly.

"You've never seen me in cold cream and curlers," she reminded him.

He rolled his eyes to the ceiling. "I hope I never do."

Big Ben looked more cheerful in the daylight, and Bergitta capriciously stuck her tongue out at him.

"He's probably the only 'man' who has ever claimed your attention at three in the morning," Jordan surmised.

She smiled enigmatically. "You would like to know, wouldn't you?"

"There are lots of things I would like to know about you, Bergitta."

They had stopped for afternoon tea at the Four Seasons, and he repeated himself. "Tell me about Bergitta," he smiled. "What was she like when she was ten, for instance?"

"Lonely. I was an only child. Afraid. My father never

had job security. Ambitious. Even at that age I felt I could do something with my life."

"And you have succeeded: I talked with the office in New York this morning. The show has brought in our highest sales ever."

A slow smile spread across Bergitta's perfectly molded features. "That's gratifying."

"Is it what you thought it would be—success, I mean?"

"I don't know. I haven't had enough of it yet."

"What? You want more?" he remarked in mock surprise.

"Of course. There's always something more. At least I feel the need for it."

"Perhaps the ambitious ten year old is still trying to prove she can make it in an adult world?"

"Is that what you think?"

"I don't know. What do you think?"

"Perhaps I am still trying to prove myself. Without my work, I can't imagine what life would be like. Probably lonely—and frightening."

Jordan smiled sympathetically. "The basic person never changes much. We all have pretty much the same needs for self-worth and acceptance."

"What about you, Jordan? I've watched you play harder than most people work. Ambition doesn't drive you. What does?"

Jordan pressed his lips together, and it was as though he pulled a mask down over his delightful, expressive face. "You wouldn't want to know the person from my past, Bergitta. He was an entirely different person."

She gave him a speculative look. "Then you are saying people *can* change."

"Sometimes they don't have a choice. Sometimes change is the only way to survive. Change is an elusive thing. Because it's a process, we can never be certain when the metamorphosis is complete, if ever."

"My father thinks change is a spiritual matter, that

80

only God can bring about a permanent change of heart and eternal destiny."

"Is that what you believe, too?"

"Yes, I believe it, but I think we largely determine our earthly destiny with the tools God gave us—intelligence, patience, hard work, and a thing called hope." She looked at him pointedly. "That's why I think it's important to do something useful with my life regardless of whether I need to produce a livelihood. It's shameful to waste life."

"Ooof!" Jordan exclaimed, clutching his stomach in a facetious reaction. "Methinks the lady lands a hard punch."

Bergitta smiled innocently. "Did I say something?"

He turned the coffee cup in his hand, and again Bergitta was entranced by his long, agile fingers. There were strength and dexterity in them. They fascinated her.

"Don't you think it's useful to head a company that provides goods to the economy and jobs to workers?"

"I certainly do. But I seem to recall that you view this as a temporary situation."

"That I do." He made a wry face. "Fashion merchandising isn't exactly my area of expertise or interest."

"What makes you tick, Jordan? What do you want from life, and what do you want to give back to it?"

He pulled an impish face. "Is that your not-so-subtle way of telling me once again that I'm a bum? Is it so bad if I've made some shrewd investments and have decided to spend the rest of my life playing? There's no law that says I have to join forces with the workaholics."

"There's something about you that tells me you're not really content with all that playing."

He covered her hand with his across the table. "You sound as though you really care, Bergitta."

"That's because I really do." She turned a melting look on him. "I have come to know you as a wonderful friend."

"Thank you for that," he said humbly. Then the corners of his eyes began to crinkle. "Better be careful, though. Involvements have been known to come out of such beginnings. Of course, I can't think of a nicer guy to get involved with than me," he teased.

What was said in jest registered as truth for Bergitta. Quietly, she said, "I can only agree with that, Jordan. You *are* a nice guy."

From that moment on, an indescribable change took place in their relationship. It was as though they had given themselves permission to explore the possibility of a deeper relationship, while remaining steadfast to the rules they had set for themselves. No longer did Jordan press her to share his bed or bedevil her with his seductions. It was as though he were content to be with her, to take delight in what delighted her, to laugh at the little things and to discuss seriously the important things.

A week passed, and a happy Bergitta finished photographic sessions in and around London. At the Changing of the Guard, she had pranced in a costume suggestive of the uniform; at the Royal Ballet, she had been gowned in the pink of a princess and crowned with a tiara and a smile for her adoring escort, Jordan. Chris caught a candid shot of the bridegroom presenting his bride with a strand of matched pearls, and this time the smiles that emanated from one to the other were not manufactured for the camera lens.

One day remained before they were to leave for the Netherlands where Bergitta would officiate at the opening of the tulip festival and pose for more photographs.

Jordan and Bergitta planned to spend that remaining day in Brighton, hopefully locating the descendants of Dr. Halstrom and returning his effects to the family. Several phone calls to the area turned up nothing. The only Halstroms listed in the telephone pages were unrelated and knew nothing of a doctor who might have served on a Red Cross ship during World War II.

"I think we should go anyway," Jordan decided. "A whole family doesn't just disappear from society. Some old-timer in the community is bound to have some clue of their whereabouts."

They boarded the train early the next morning. It was more than an hour's ride to the seaside resort of Brighton. The incoming trains were loaded with commuters coming into the city to work, but the trains going out to Brighton were nearly empty.

The late spring air was brisk, and the nearer they came to the small city that had once begun as a fishing village, the more they could smell the earth and sea.

Jordan struck up a conversation with a train porter who happened to live in Brighton and inquired if there might be an old family-owned pharmacy in the city that had been in operation for at least fifty years. The old gentleman gave him the names of two, and Jordan jotted the addresses down on a notepad.

"That was a stroke of genius," Bergitta said admiringly, as the porter went on his way.

"We'll see. If anyone would remember a Dr. Halstrom, it would most likely be someone who had filled his prescriptions."

The first address had recently modernized and changed hands. Bergitta and Jordan were quickly told that records as old as the ones they sought would long ago have been destroyed. There was no street by the name of the second address given, Benson Way. After a few fruitless inquiries, Jordan decided to go to the Hall of Records and look at an old city map. An elderly clerk remembered the name and explained that the city streets had been renamed into avenues and boulevards and that only a few elderly residents still used the original names. She assisted Jordan in locating the street's new name.

The faded gold letters on the door could barely be made out: Benson Way Pharmaceutical and Sundries. A bell tinkled as they entered the quaint shop that appeared to have been left untouched for fifty years. A young man with a mop of curly blond hair and wearing a white uniform coat greeted them. Jordan briefly explained that he had reason to try to make contact with the family of Dr. Walter C. Halstrom and wondered if someone from this concern might have known him.

"Halstrom...Halstrom." The pharmacist scratched his head. "I went to school with a chap named Halstrom. He was several years ahead of me and went to the medical school. I don't know if his father was a doctor, though. I think he may have gone down with a ship during the war. His mum never remarried."

"That could possibly be the one," Jordan said with mounting hope. "Do you by any chance remember where young Halstrom set up practice, or at least the medical school he attended?"

"No." Then the fair face brightened. "My grandfather might, though. He knew every bloke around here." He went to the phone and put the question to the old man on the other end of the line. Momentarily he turned the receiver over to Jordan who asked terse questions and listened intensely to the answers. He thanked the pharmacist for his help, and he and Bergitta left to seek the address in the hired car.

"The son lives in the original resort area down by the sea," Jordan explained as he maneuvered the car expertly through the streets to a place called Camden Corners.

A pretty young woman answered the door. She was carrying a baby and holding a two-year-old by the hand.

"Hello, my name is Jordan Worthington, and this is my wife Bergitta. Might this be the residence of a Dr. Halstrom whose father was Dr. Walter C. Halstrom?" Jordan inquired.

"Who is it, Millie?" a voice behind her inquired. A dark-haired man in a wheelchair rolled himself to the door. His face was etched with pain and bitterness.

"This is Mr. Worthington and his wife, Paul. They would like to speak with you," the sunny dispositioned woman said.

"What about?" Dr. Halstrom growled rudely. "We're not receiving callers this morning," he craned his head around his wife to tell Jordan.

"I'm sorry we couldn't reach you by phone. Your number was unlisted. We have traveled from London, and I think you will find it in your interest to give us a few minutes of your time," Jordan said firmly.

Reluctantly Paul signaled his wife to let them enter.

"What is it that you've got there?" the wheelchair victim scowled as Jordan placed the leather pouch on the table. Jordan turned the bag so that Paul Halstrom could see the initials.

The doctor squenched his eyes and scrutinized the gold letters disbelievingly. No one spoke in the stunned quiet.

"It was your father's," Jordan said calmly, sensing the need to discharge the tension in the atmosphere.

Paul picked up the stiff leather object and turned it slowly in his hands. "Where did you get it?" he cried hoarsely.

Jordan crossed the short distance between them and in an act of compassion laid his hand on the man's shoulder. "I am a diver of sorts. Not too far off the coast of England I was doing some diving inside a rock formation. I had heard through diving circles that wreckage was suspected to have been carried there by the currents. Miraculously, I found an entire section intact, and the bag was lodged in an air pocket of what appeared to have been a medical supplies storage closet. This was the only object that was salvageable. I thought you would like to have it."

Suddenly the man clutched the case to his breast and began to heave great sobs. Jordan motioned to Bergitta, and they began to tiptoe across the room toward the front door.

"Don't go!" the grieving son called out. "Please stay."

As Jordan and Bergitta came back to take the chairs Mrs. Halstrom offered, her husband said, "I haven't had the opportunity to thank you—or to apologize for my abominable rudeness."

"Paul hasn't been himself since his accident left him paralyzed from the waist down," his wife said.

Jordan nodded understandingly. "It takes time to get over these things."

"Get *over* it?" Paul exclaimed in astonishment. "How does one get over a lost career? My father was the lucky one. At least he was able to die with his career."

In anguish, the young wife tried to silence her husband. Jordan quickly perceived the inner turmoil that gripped the young family. He looked directly at Paul.

"It's your legs that are paralyzed—not your career."

"And what would *you* know about it? Do you know how important mobility is to a doctor? Do you know how much a patient's confidence relies on a doctor's own robust good health?"

"I might," Jordan said mildly. "There is more than one kind of handicap, and I know something about that. You can't give up."

"But I—"

"Open the case," Jordan ordered.

Paul Halstrom did so, handling the instruments of medicine one by one.

"Your hands still work. They are not paralyzed. They are a doctor's best tools."

Bergitta's eyes flew to Jordan's hands reposed on his knees and then to his face. He was talking from self-knowledge. She felt it intuitively. But how? What handicap was he speaking of? What career?

Paul was listening intently to Jordan now, and the thread that linked them was a fragile life line to hope.

"Some of the finest work in medicine has been done by physicians whose own health has in some way been impaired. In some, the disability merely seems to in-

86

spire them. If you feel there is no potential for a patient practice, there are other fields in medicine, such as research."

"It would take additional training. It would mean starting over."

"So what? You're young enough to start over."

Paul turned the case over and over on his lap, stroking it gently. "My grandfather made a present of this to my father on the day he graduated from med school. My grandfather was also a physician. I come from a long line of men in the medical profession."

Jordan smiled. "I hope this isn't the end of the line."

Paul was thoughtful. "Maybe not. Perhaps the last real measure of devotion I could pay my father is to put his bag to work again."

Paul's wife was ecstatic. "Please stay a little longer. I'll make some tea."

Bergitta took over the two youngsters while Mary Halstrom was busy in the kitchen. Jordan watched her there on the floor, stacking the toy blocks until they toppled and squealing with the little ones as they crashed. He was captivated by a side of her he had never seen before. Instead of the sophisticated successful designer, he was seeing a carefree, fun-loving little girl. Her childlike vulnerability made her more appealing than ever.

He turned his attention to Paul who was explaining the details of his permanent injury in technical terms.

Bergitta listened with one ear. She didn't understand the medical terminology at all, but Jordan seemed to follow easily, even interjecting several intelligent questions and comments.

Mary brought in a silver tray laid with crisp linen napkins and graced by a long slender rose in a bud vase. Fragrant tea, served in thin bone china cups, was accompanied by fresh-baked tarts.

Mary's face glowed with pleasure as Bergitta complimented the elegant setting. "We have friends in so seldom. It is a treat to use my nice things," she said with a poignant note in her voice.

An hour later they left Paul Halstrom formulating plans to revitalize his career. He rolled his chair to see them to the door and raised grateful eyes to Jordan. "I think Providence must have sent you." He held up the black bag. "Thank you for the gift."

In the rented car Bergitta felt tears in her eyes as they drove along the curving road by the seaside. "What you gave him was more than a family heirloom. You gave him back the gift of his dignity and usefulness—you gave him back his life!" Suddenly all that had been involved in getting the case to Paul Halstrom dawned on Bergitta—the dangerous dive, the tedious search to find the Halstrom son, the time and effort used to deliver the family treasure, and then the care that went into helping this stranger come to grips with his own courage.

"Why did you do it, Jordan? The willingness to become involved in someone's life just doesn't exist anymore, yet you left him your card and a copy of your itinerary if he needed to reach you. Why?"

Jordan didn't answer immediately. It was as though his thoughts were captivated by another time and place. Then he sighed and said matter of factly, "Perhaps, Bergitta, it was because someone once did that for me."

She waited for him to go on, but he didn't. He pulled the car over into a municipal beach area where the music was loud and the crowds were thick. "This isn't ideal, but we can get a bite of lunch at the Emporium."

The jostling crowds were noisy, and group after group stopped at the couple's patio table with invitations to go windsurfing. Bergitta wanted to scream. She wanted to know more about Jordan and the elusive secrets of his past. But this was no place for conversation. This crowd wanted action!

"How about it, Bergitta? Shall we 'ave a go?" He

grinned at his successful mimicking of the "bloke" who had just left their table.

She shook her head. "I don't think so. My beach bag is back at the hotel. You go ahead, though."

"I think I can rustle up something to wear from the beach concession," he said and sauntered off to outfit himself.

It was a glorious, balmy day, Bergitta noted, as she looked out across the deep to where the ocean became as blue as sapphires at the horizon. It was an artist's sky with cirrus formations piled into great humps. In fact, there were several artists on the beach, and Bergitta took a stroll to glimpse the work on their easels.

All nodded their heads and lifted hands in greeting. It was interesting to observe what each artist took from the scene. One canvas was filled with gliding gulls and had successfully interpreted their free-spirited flight. Another brought the clouds to canvas but painted them as stormy over a tempestuous sea. An elderly man transferred the playing children to canvas. From the sparkle in his eye and the enthusiasm with which he smiled and waved, their verve seemed to restore his own youth.

She stuffed her hands into the ample pockets of the loose, swingy pink linen dress she wore and thought how interesting were the subject choices in the paintings. Each artist had seen the same scene, yet each had taken a different conception from it. How like life that was. She had looked at life and had chosen to pursue career goals. Paul Halstrom had met tragedy in life and had taken defeat from it. Jordan had chosen "the good life"—but was it really "good"? She watched him glide across the surf against the wind-driven sail. He was expert at it, of course, as he was at everything else he set about.

He was an enigma. Photos in cosmopolitan magazines portrayed him as someone whose only goal in life was to raise his glass in toast to the world at play, and Bergitta had expected she would have to go along with him to an extent during the tour. Surprisingly enough, there had been none of that. In fact, he had even seemed to avoid those scenes. Could she have been wrong about him? Perhaps it was Clare who demanded the nightlife because she needed the spotlight for her career.

She walked on along, her deep-auburn hair swinging free in the breeze and blowing about her creamy complexion, which was tinted just enough by the sun to give her face a ripened glow. She paused to watch an artist work who was very proficient in water colors. He was fast—as one *had* to be when using water colors, and there was bold brilliance in his depiction of the sea.

She pointed to Jordan's figure windsurfing on the sea and made arrangements with the artist to paint him for a fee. She stayed to watch as the swift strokes of the brush brought to life the surfer's superb physique mastering the sea on his red and white windsurfing rig.

When the artist was finished, he placed the painting in a pre-cut mat he had with him and folded a large sheet of water color paper to make an envelope for it. Bergitta paid him, delighted with the painting, and quickly tucked it into her carryall as she saw Jordan approaching.

He lifted his arms over his head and clasped his hands in a victory signal, grinning broadly.

She waved a welcome. "I saw you out there cutting through the wind," she smiled, her emerald eyes sparkling a reflection of his own enthusiasm. "You were great."

"I got a pretty good crosswind a time or two. That makes it exciting!" He tucked her arm through his as they walked back to the car. "I saw you 'hunkering down' behind the artists. I figured you were probably getting lonesome for the old sketch pad."

"I am," Bergitta admitted. "Do you know I actually have not picked it up since I left New York?"

Jordan squeezed her arm. "Good. You needed a vaca-

tion. Maybe you have found some other things to interest you besides the challenge of that blank piece of
paper?" His eyes looked at her wickedly.

"Such as?" she said with a scornful lift of her chin,
but the twinkle in her eye gave him the clue that she ca-
pitulated to the point.

On the train back to London she slept peacefully
while he rifled through some papers and made prepara-
tion for a business lunch with an investment brokerage
firm he was investigating for the purpose of retaining
their services. It seemed no time before they were back
at the hotel.

Chapter Six

At six o'clock that evening Bergitta was rested and refreshed, and she fell right in with Jordan's plans. He suggested they eat at one of London's famous restaurants known for its excellent beef Wellington. Then they could go on to the late spots after dinner.

Bergitta hummed happily in the shower and marveled at her pink-cheeked excitement as she applied foundation for her makeup. She tingled at the prospect of another wonderful evening with Jordan and tried to still the fluttering inside her. "It's only a date," she reminded herself. "Who else would he go out with? It means nothing to him. This will all be over in a few weeks." But no matter how stern she was with herself, her anticipation only mounted higher.

Jordan came in to help her with her wrap and to admire the eggplant-purple, moire taffeta creation she was wearing. "It makes your eyes look deep and mysterious," he said softly, planting a kiss on her supple, flowing locks that curved around her face the way he liked.

He was resplendent in a black tuxedo, and it was all Bergitta could do to restrain an impulse to reach out and stroke the strong, muscular arms.

Dazzling brass, tiffany lamps, stained-glass windows, and polished wood were reminiscent of turn-of-the-century elegance in the small restaurant. They were seated and an unobtrusive waiter brought them a wine list.

"No thanks," Jordan shook his head and ordered Perrier for both of them. They sipped on their water and settled back in their curtained booth to study the menu.

Bergitta looked up to find that Jordan was studying *her*. She smiled at him and nodded toward the ignored menu. "You're not going to be ready to order when the waiter comes back. There are some delectable dishes here."

He continued to study her. "I have the most delectable dish I could imagine." He reached across the table and enclosed her hand in his. His thumb began to stroke her palm in a gentle circular motion while his eyes never left hers. A warm tremor spread through her stomach and blossomed into butterflies. They fluttered a feathery dance up her spine, then flew dizzily around in her head. What was Jordan doing to her? His teasing caresses of her hand created an urgency, and she slid her fingers between his until they were intertwined in a locking embrace. She saw the deepening emotion in his face and thrilled to know that she had the power to create in him the same ecstasy she was feeling.

"This wasn't in the plan," she whispered.

The timbre of his voice stirred deeper excitement in her as he replied, "The best things in life often *are* unplanned—like an adventure that takes you from one plateau to the next higher one. You take what is wonderful and good from it." His grip tightened. "You are wonderful and good," he said huskily.

"But I'm not for the taking," she reminded him, seeming suddenly to remember a danger in this relationship.

He drew her hand to his lips and held it there for a moment. "I know your plan, Bergitta. You want the rainbow and both pots of gold at the ends of it. The rainbow is a mirage and the pot of gold is a myth. I can't give you rainbows, Bergitta, but I can put stars in your eyes."

She had no doubt of that judging from the starbursts that he had already detonated. Jordan had an attraction that she had not ever discovered in another man. That he had this much power to make her senses do his bidding was frightening. She fought off the growing conviction that he was beginning to play too important a role in her life. In hopes of regaining some control, she removed her hand from his. Undaunted, he continued to romance her with his eyes, making seductive inquiries over her body as his eyes shot sparks of passion like splintered diamonds.

Her breath was coming in uneven spurts, and she feverishly sought a safe topic of conversation. "Windsurfing looks like fun. Is it difficult to learn?"

"Not if you are a natural athlete and are accomplished at other water sports."

"Well, you were in fine form today. You were magnificent."

"I play to an audience," he said softly, "especially when the audience is you."

She laughed uneasily. "Who are you kidding? You were perfectly aware that the entire beach stopped to watch your performance. You loved the attention," she teasingly accused. "But then, I suppose we all do. That's part of our nature, isn't it? I like recognition when I've done good design work."

"You are made for a man to lavish attention on, Bergitta. But no man wants to feel he is being fit into your list of priorities somewhere between your career and doing the laundry."

She bristled. "And you can speak for the entire male contingency?"

"I think I know my species pretty well."

The waiter came, and not a moment too soon, Bergitta decided.

They ate in silence, Bergitta musing that an entirely

new Jordan had come into focus these past weeks. His personal magnetism both frightened and attracted her.

After dinner they went on to a place called the Wit's End Players, where a comedy group specialized in short skits and off-beat humor. They threw themselves into the gala atmosphere and merged into the spirit of the fun-loving crowd.

Finally they left there and went on to a place Jordan knew that specialized in musical satire. The Knight Club with its musical group called Knights of the Round Table was just as much fun as Jordan had promised. The ballads were performed with authenticity and musical integrity, and the ribald humor stayed in the bounds of good taste.

It was a fun evening. More than once Jordan had drawn her close to him in a gesture of oneness that they were sharing this special time together. She was reluctant to give up the magic, but at last she relinquished the spell.

She yawned. "I want to go to the hotel now, Jordan."

He smiled at her sleepiness.

"I have something for you back at the hotel," she surprised him by saying as they rode in the cab.

He cocked an eyebrow. "Sounds interesting."

She blushed as she caught onto his unmistakable inuendo. "I have a *present* for you, Jordan," she clarified indignantly, "and it certainly isn't me!"

He had his laugh and said, "A pity. You hold a strong defense, Bergitta."

"I have to if I want to win the war." Grasping at an opportunity to change the subject, she added, "Did you ever serve with the military?"

Suddenly he became quiet, muttering almost unintelligibly that he had done a brief tour.

"What outfit were you in?" she persisted, aiming to stay on safe ground.

From the wrinkled forehead and twitching corners of

his mouth, she knew he was about to give a nonsensical answer.

"I believe the outfit I was in was drab green trimmed with brass buttons, ribbons, and gold braid. Personally, I thought they overdid the gold braid," he finished, his eyes crinkling with laughter.

"You can take your tongue out of your cheek now," Bergitta said acidly. "You have made your point. If you don't want to talk about your military career, that's fine."

"I don't, Bergitta," he said soberly. "There are some things that just don't make good conversation, and that part of my past is definitely in that category." The subject was closed. It was his turn to divert the conversation.

"So you have a gift for me," he mused. She could tell he was intrigued. "Is it mineral, vegetable, or animal?" he coaxed her.

"None of the above," she said smugly, deciding to be as evasive as he.

"Ah, c'mon. That defies all the laws of physics."

"Mmmmm, okay then," her eyes twinkled, "it's a little of all three."

"You're an exasperating woman, you know it?" he growled, and he fell silent until they reached the hotel.

At the door of their suite, Jordan inserted the key into the lock, then paused. "I'd better do this here. I don't trust myself inside." He bent and kissed her lightly. "This one is not for the camera." His kiss became deeply passionate.

She looked up at him through the long lashes that curtained her large eyes. "Thank you for a lovely evening, Jordan. It was delightful."

He started to say something, changed his mind, then bent and kissed her on the tip of the nose before ushering her inside.

While Jordan waited in the sitting room, Bergitta unzipped her dress, stepped out of it in a graceful long-legged motion, and hung it in her closet, at the same time taking down her blue satin robe and slipping into it. She showered under a gentle stream, like falling spring rain, relaxing in its warmth. She toweled dry and changed into silk lounging pajamas the color of rich cream before going out to join Jordan for their usual nightcap. On her way out, she picked up the envelope containing the water color and went into the sitting room that separated her sleeping quarters from Jordan's.

As he mixed their drinks, he stole glances at her reclining on the burgundy velvet couch, her tiny feet, clad in dainty high-heeled bedroom slippers, tucked up beside her. He handed her one of the tonic waters laced with a mixture of fruit elixirs. She noticed he had used no alcohol from the well-stocked bar.

Bergitta sipped on hers, her long, slender, pink-tipped fingers curling around the icy glass. The concoction was delicious.

"You don't drink much, do you, Jordan?" Her lowered lashes veiled the brilliant green pools that captured his eyes over the edge of the glass.

"Correction. I don't drink at all." He sat down, then moved her feet to his lap.

Since he didn't elaborate, she went on to present the envelope. "Something for you. I hope you'll like it."

"I'm sure I shall, since I like the giver." His eyes smiled at her. "But there must have been something to prompt the gift."

"Yes," she agreed, "I saw you give a man's life back to him today, Jordan, and I was moved by it. Until today, I had never understood your free-spirited living. I found myself understanding that this was the key to your helping Paul Halstrom. You had the uninhibited persistence to go after the unknown. I respect that, and this is something that captures that part of you."

More intrigued than ever, he opened the envelope and discovered the likeness of himself. He studied the painting. The artist had faithfully portrayed his virile form and vibrant, indomitable spirit. It was all there—the qualities of enduring strength, keen skill, and raw courage.

"Your artist had quite an imagination," he laughed modestly.

"No. He painted what he saw. I saw the same thing." His eyes burned into hers. "Bergitta—"

"May I also apologize for certain unfair remarks I have made in the past?"

They both knew she was referring to the heated accusations that had begun their relationship during J.W.'s illness.

"Bergitta, there was so much we didn't know about each other then. Every day I discover some new delight about you, right down to your delectable pink toes." His fingers playfully tickled the tiny appendages that peeked through the satin open-toed slippers beside him. She wriggled her feet, squealing in protest. He looked at her in happy astonishment. "You're ticklish!"

"No—I'm *not!*" Her hands held him off as she saw the mischievous intent in his movement toward her. In a moment she was helpless under his playful assault which sent her into a crumpled heap amid spasms of shrieking giggles. Gasping for breath, she pleaded with him to stop. He did, but the surge of excitement lingered, and suddenly they found themselves swept into a passionate centripetal force, unable to break loose from the whirling magnetic attraction that threatened to merge them in its power.

He drew back. "I don't dare touch you," he breathed. Holding himself in rigid control, he lowered his lips to hers, tasting the sweetness and the innocence there. "Go to bed, Bergitta," he said roughly, his eyes burning with desire.

"Goodnight, Jordan." She rose, dropped a kiss on his forehead, and walked lissomely to her bedroom.

They were awakened the next morning by a tap at the door. Bergitta and Jordan appeared at the same time in their dressing gowns to answer it.

"I waited until two a.m. for you two to get in," Chris Jamison complained. It was obvious that he was teeming with excitement.

"Get to the point, Jamison," Jordan snapped irritably, standing aside and motioning the photographer in.

"You'll never believe this!" he declared exuberantly, including them both in his gaze. "*I* don't even believe this! We have an invitation to meet for a photographic session and interview with a prominent designer often commissioned by the royal family to do special-occasion clothes. A photographer friend who has contacts with the palace arranged it. He owed me a favor." Chris beamed from one to the other. "It's not on the agenda, but what do you think? Should we go for it?"

The rest of the morning was spent getting ready. Questions unique to a palace designer had to be formulated and the poses planned. Finally they were finished, and Jordan saw Chris to the door. He turned back to Bergitta after closing the door and winked gleefully. "Didn't I tell you he was good at his job?"

"Yes, that was quite a coup," Bergitta smiled. "Everyone will gain by it." A frown creased her brow. "But, Jordan, there seems to be something between you two—a rift or something. I can feel it. It's almost a hindrance to our working together as a team."

"Nonsense. Shall I have lunch sent up, or would you like to go out?"

Annoyed by his rebuff, she shook her head. "Neither. I have some work to do."

He shrugged. "So be it." He turned on his heel to disappear into the bathroom.

The next day they waited in a rather plain salon for the famous London designer to appear. At last Grayson Thatcher of Grayson's, Inc., presented himself and extended both hands in a warm greeting to Bergitta, informing her at once that he had seen and appreciated her work on the wedding line at a recent showing. She nodded a polite acceptance of his compliment and told him that she was an admirer of his work, too. They lapsed into shop talk as he showed her through his establishment and offered her several of his latest designs to look at. All the while Chris was shooting one photo right after the other. Jordan looked mildly bored and was glad to stay in the background.

When Bergitta probed about his work for Buckingham Palace, he shook his head sadly. His thin nose almost seemed to sharpen. "Ah, so sadly, I cannot keep up with all the work I have. Now the princess is requesting that I do a wardrobe for the little four-year-old daughter. Unfortunately, designing for children is not my specialty. That is something you would be better at," he smiled at Bergitta.

"I would be delighted," she smiled back, her breath quickening.

"Indeed?" The middle-aged designer scrutinized her across gold-rimmed spectacles, and after satisfying himself that she was serious, he asked a few more questions. Then he launched into a description of occasions the clothes would be needed for and the tastes of his client. He suggested that if she would have some trial designs ready for him to approve within a month, he would personally present them to the princess.

Bergitta was ecstatic. She left walking on the proverbial cloud nine. "I can't believe my good fortune," she caroled, and she thanked Chris profusely for arranging the interview.

"That's the name of the game!" he chortled. "Fame and fortune!"

Jordan offered his congratulations but otherwise was silent.

When they reached the hotel, Bergitta called Bernie in New York and asked her assistant to start doing some research on what the fashion scene was projecting for children's clothing the next season. Then she sent for Libby, and they cloistered themselves in her room, discussing fabrics and techniques that might apply specifically to children's wear.

Libby had barely left in the late afternoon, when Bernie called with the information she had gathered. After the exchange, Bernie asked in an attempt at casualness, "By the way, how are you and Jordan getting on?" Bergitta burbled enthusiastically about how she had found a new friend in Jordan and had discovered he was not at all the person she had misjudged him to be. There was a slight hesitation. Then Bernie said, "Go slowly, B. G. Things may not be as simple as they seem to be."

Bergitta tensed, at once alert. "What do you mean?"

"I mean that there is a rumor circulating to the effect that all is not over between Jordan and Clare L'aimant."

"Oh." Bergitta's voice drooped.

She hung up the phone, her hand remaining on the receiver as she gave Bernie's warning deep thought. Had Jordan lied to her after all? Were his attempts to love her merely a pastime to use her as a stand-in bride while he waited for Clare? What was going on?

She declined his invitation to dinner, claiming to be too tired from the day's concentrated work.

"Perhaps it's just as well," he shrugged. "We have an early flight for Amsterdam tomorrow."

Chapter Seven

The tranquil visit to Amsterdam was refreshing after the mad dash around London's streets. Jordan and Bergitta arrived at eight in the morning, and Dutch housewives had long since finished the daily ritual of scrubbing their marble stoops until they shone in the glistening sunlight. Bergitta exclaimed over the wreaths and door pieces fashioned from spring flowering bulbs. They decorated the front entrances of nearly every home and business.

Bergitta was fascinated as they rode past the canals on the way to the hotel from the airport. The windmills were huge affairs compared to the prairie variety of windmill she had seen as a child in her native state of Iowa. These were huge buildings! Their paddles continually operated the pumps that drained the polders, keeping the reclaimed flat lands from once again being swamped by the sea. Boats were negotiating the canals as traffic would the streets.

Heiberscham, their escort for the tulip festival, showed them to the VIP suite of the hotel. The room overlooked the colorful city with its network of canals and beautifully laid out tulip gardens.

Before he left, Heiberscham provided Bergitta and Jordan with a schedule of events and their itinerary while they were guests of the city. "Tomorrow, your float will lead the parade, and at the end of it, you and your bride will officially proclaim the opening of the festival in a ceremony at the central gardens," the stocky blond-haired man told them. He walked to the closet. "We have provided a national costume that is the traditional wedding attire for our country. Would you honor us by wearing it in the parade?"

Bergitta gasped at the lovely creation he laid across the bed for her inspection. It was styled along the lines of a peasant costume with a tightly laced vest in white velvet over a dirndl skirt of satin with lace-edged ruffles. A veil of illusion flowed from a white cap with a cuff pointed in true Dutch style. The entire outfit was heavily braided and embroidered with silk floss and seed pearls. Jordan's costume was also white with a short jacket, embroidered lapels, and a wide cummerbund of white satin.

"We will be delighted and complimented," Bergitta smiled in a way that dazzled him.

"Speak for yourself," Jordan growled after he had closed the door behind Heiberscham. He tried on the wide-brimmed felt hat embellished with pearl-studded braid and scowled into the mirror.

Bergitta squealed with delight at his dour expression. "Where is your spirit of adventure?" she taunted as he stated his intention to duck out on the parade.

"I've never had to dodge rotten eggs and tomatoes yet, and I don't intend to start now!" he stated firmly. "This whole thing is so hokey it smells."

Bergitta's temper flared. "It wasn't my idea, if you recall! You and Clare planned the big-time wedding scene."

"I meant nothing personal, Bergitta." He studied her covertly and then said broodingly, "Perhaps it's because you are so real that I find this whole charade so deplorable—while I find you more and more adorable." He crossed the room to where she was standing, still holding the wedding garment in her hands. He tipped her chin and looked into her eyes. "I'm so sorry to put you through this, Bergitta," he whispered, dropping a gentle hand to her cheek and caressing it with the backs of his fingers. "If we can hang in for another month, it'll be over."

Why didn't it sound good to her? Why wasn't she anxious to be back in her nest in New York—her own little design studio? Why did the thought of being without Jordan leave an empty lost feeling?

"C'mon. We've got the day. Let's have some fun."

Jordan knew how to do just that, as Bergitta learned more and more every day. They took a sightseeing tour on a canal boat. Once they were out in the countryside, Jordan entertained her with exaggerated imitations of canal boatmen singing ridiculous songs of the sea. He threatened to pull her overboard with him if he lost his balance.

They docked the boat at a small group of pilings, and Jordan lifted her off onto land. A trail led to a thicket of trees, and on the other side of a rise was the most glorious sight Bergitta had ever seen. Fields of tulips grew in colorful patches of red, blue, purple, yellow, pink and orange, all in neat squares like a great patchwork quilt covering the earth.

"I shall never forget this moment as long as I live," Bergitta said appreciatively. Seeing her face glowing so alive with joy, Jordan knew he never would either.

"Such natural grandeur makes my own efforts at creating beauty seem insignificant by comparison," the designer said ruefully. "It puts an inflated self-importance back into perspective, doesn't it?" she smiled. "A handful of earth, a bulb that sits and does nothing, some rain and sunshine, and *voila*—a miracle." She stooped and plucked a rare blue tulip that exactly matched the blue of the linen dress she wore.

"It's the proper balance of all those properties that makes it happen," Jordan added to her oversimplification. "The right amounts of everything produce a chemistry that makes the right thing happen." He turned her to him. "We have the right chemistry, Bergitta. Our personalities balance each other. We have the right mix to make something wonderfully productive happen."

She surrendered to his kiss. How could anyone so wonderful possibly be as untrue as Bernie had suggested? Her heart wanted to deny any credibility in the rumors her assistant had heard. Yet a small part of her reserved room for doubt. There was a lot she didn't know about him, and he wasn't willing to open up the pages of his past.

Bergitta withdrew from his embrace, and hand in hand they strolled down the paths between the neatly kept beds of tulips.

"What you just said is the combination for life itself," Bergitta commented. "If we are going to be productive, we must find the right balance between work, play, expanding our horizons, and giving to others. We all owe a contribution to our planet, don't you think?"

She had stopped, and he was looking at her earnestly. He twirled a finger around a curl near her earlobe. "If you say so," he returned noncommittally.

They stayed to watch a spectacular sunset that vividly reproduced every shade of the colorful fields of flowers. Bergitta exhaled a deep sigh as they reluctantly turned their steps to the boat still moored at the pilings. As usual Jordan had provided an entertaining afternoon, but deep in her heart she knew that his presence had been at least half the joy. Without him to share it with, her pleasure would have been incomplete.

The next afternoon Chris claimed their time with more publicity shots. There were more fields of tulips in which Bergitta and Jordan wandered hand in hand, but this time for the camera. "Budding Love Blossoms" was the theme the publicity department of Design House had chosen for the Holland tour. Bergitta posed in a white, simple design accessorized with varying scarves, sashes, and functional extras in the purity of tulip colors. Always there was the admiring husband in the background for the benefit of those incurable romantics who would read the fashion magazines.

The love scenes were becoming more and more natural. It was no longer a strain to be kissed by Jordan, even in front of the camera. For Bergitta, as the moment more and more often took on reality, she began to suspect that her feelings for Jordan were greater than she wanted to risk.

Shots were made at windmills, on the canal boats, and in the city. By the time costumes were changed with the help of faithful Libby, the entire afternoon was gone.

The sun had set when they arrived back at the hotel. A gala dinner dance would be held that evening in their honor in the ballroom of the hotel where they were staying. It was part of the prefestival activity.

Bergitta dressed for it in a casual manner, relishing the extra hour to sink into the jacuzzi and allow the pummeling waters to pelt her muscles into relaxation. She heard Jordan moving around in the next room, and an unbidden thought entered her mind. If the marriage were real, how cozy it would be to share these luxurious moments with someone she loved.

She rose from the bath and wrapped herself in an oversized towel just as Jordan came in with a towel draped around his middle. She carefully averted her eyes as he lowered himself into the bubbling water.

"You might at least have given me warning that you intended to use the jacuzzi. I would gladly have vacated the premises," she said huffily, gathering up her cosmetic case and blow dryer.

Jordan cast her an amused smile. "It's difficult for me to adjust to such modesty in a woman in this day and time. No doubt your religious upbringing has something to do with your inhibitions."

Bergitta paused at the doorway as she was leaving.

"Inhibition has nothing to do with it, religious or otherwise. I simply do not choose to share intimacies with anyone other than the one I'll share the rest of my life with."

Jordan regarded her solemnly. "Whoever that may be, he'll be the luckiest guy in the world."

Back in her room, Bergitta slid into the dress designed especially for this event at her own drawing board. Large three-dimensional tulip cups rose from a narrow waist to blossom full over the bosom, their pointed petals forming an irregular line at the top of the strapless bodice. The varying shades of pink tulips reflected a glow in the clear, fresh complexion of the wearer. A border of intertwined tulips formed the scalloped ankle-length hemline, also in pink, with green tulip blades hand-appliquéd in satin in the same manner as the blossoms.

Bergitta rang for Libby to come and check for any final imperfection such as a loose thread or a pulled stitch, as was their custom. The high-tech camera faithfully recorded even the slightest flaw, and Design House quality had to be protected with the closest scrutiny.

Libby stood back and squinted critically. "The hairstyle is right, but something is missing." She stepped quickly to the vase of tulips on the occasional table and chose four in slender pink bud. Three, she wound around into the braided chignon pulled tightly to the back of Bergitta's head; the other, she handed to Bergitta to carry along with her pink satin evening purse which exactly matched her shoes.

"Perfect!" a voice said.

They looked up to see Jordan standing in the doorway that connected the room with the rest of the suite. He was smiling, his eyes softly brilliant as he took pleasure in her beauty.

Bergitta returned his smile, all annoyance from their earlier conversation gone. "Those are pretty nice threads you're wearing yourself." Her eyes traveled the length and breadth of his arrow-straight body. The impeccably tailored gray tuxedo scarcely concealed the superb muscle tone that molded against the fabric. Her heart began to pound within her at just the sight of him. Feeling that he and Libby both must be hearing the drumbeat, she stepped to the door. "Shall we go?"

Libby had decided not to join them for the evening, so the two went on alone. In the elevator Jordan bent and kissed her unexpectedly.

"Just practicing my part," he grinned as Bergitta stepped back in surprise. "I believe it's called the warm-up before the main event!"

"You really enjoy playing the part of the ardent husband for the benefit of our public, don't you?" Her irritation was thinly concealed.

"Who said I was play-acting?" he answered promptly. "And it's not the public's benefit I had in mind." His eyes twinkled at her flustered reaction. "There! That's more like a bride should look," he encouraged, pulling her deliberately into his arms and kissing her fully as the elevator doors slid open.

Photographers were there awaiting their arrival and were rewarded by finding their subjects locked in each other's arms.

Huge bowls of tulips in carnival colors decorated the dinner tables laid with white linen. There were humorous speeches, mostly in Dutch with an occasional comment in English out of courtesy to the American guests of honor. The food was delectable, and Bergitta truly regretted the evening's finish when they all stood, joined hands, and sang the festival's theme song.

Heiberscham leaned over from his place next to Jordan and Bergitta. "Would you like to have a look at the floats that are being decorated for the parade tomorrow? They will be working all night so that the flowers will be spectacularly fresh for the judging. This will give you an opportunity to see the float you will be presented on," he said with a thick accent.

Spectacular was the right description, Bergitta decided, as they entered the immense warehouse arena where the floats were being put together by many, many hands. They were taken to the lead float—the one that was especially designed for the American visitors who would act as grand marshals of the parade.

Bergitta clasped her hands in excitement at the multi-tiered wedding cake covered with rows of satin ruching to resemble the traditional frosting. Tulip bouquets were fastened in scalloped ropes around the edge of each cake layer. At the top there was a pedestal where the bride and groom would stand—Bergitta and Jordan.

Bergitta felt him stiffen when he realized this, but he said nothing. As always he was the competent and courteous company representative.

A section of the float opened for a doorway. Heiberscham took them inside so they could see the stairway they would mount to the upper pedestal. Also there was the Jeep that would drive the wedding cake float down the three-mile parade route.

Heiberscham smiled and said to them, "This float is not in the official competition. It has already been given the special award of merit by virtue of it's good-will mission from our country to yours. The ribbon will be presented to you both at the judges' stand tomorrow when you make the proclamation opening the festivities." He handed them a long scroll. "This is what you will read." Later in the hotel room Bergitta sat on the gold Victorian love seat scanning the scroll to familiarize herself with the terminology. Room service had delivered a pot of specially blended tea with croissants and jam which were now sitting on the coffee table.

A soft rain was falling. Jordan came from the shower, still toweling his hair dry and wrapped in a cinnamon shade bathrobe. "Perhaps it will rain on our parade," he said with a touch of irony.

"You wish," Bergitta quipped as she poured a cup of the hot fragrant liquid for him.

He sat on the seat beside her. "Rain or no rain, I am not posing on top of that float tomorrow." The statement was flat and final.

Bergitta laughed nervously. "I don't think you would want to put Design House in the position of failing to cooperate with our host."

"I didn't say Design House wouldn't be represented. *You* can ride on the float."

Bergitta winced at the expletives that followed his remark.

"That's not how it's done," she began, her mouth pulled tight. "Wedding cakes have both a bride and a groom at the top."

"This one isn't going to," Jordan declared. "Did the publicity department know this was part of the plan?"

"Clare approved it," Bergitta nodded sweetly.

Jordan scowled. "I suppose I should be a good scout and go along with it."

"I suppose," she agreed, releasing a breath in relief.

"I didn't say I was going to," he warned.

"Of course not," she said equably and felt it best to change the subject. "Tell me about the trip you have planned for skiing in the Alps."

"Correction. The ski trip *we* have planned."

"I had nothing to do with it. I don't like to ski and I'm afraid of heights." She paused. "Besides, it's not on the itinerary."

"You don't like to ski because you've never tried. Where's your spirit of adventure?"

"About the same place yours is in regard to the parade tomorrow."

"Ouch!" he yelped. "Pull in your claws."

Jordan was laughing, but Bergitta wasn't amused. This husband of hers was deadly serious about accepting challenges requiring the nerves of a daredevil. It seemed he lived on the edge of danger.

"This room is like something out of a fairy tale, isn't it?" Her gaze swept the room with its gold damask drapes that matched the upholstered furniture. A white thick carpet covered most of the floor except for a margin of blue delft tile—the same tile that decorated the cozy little fireplace in which a fire burned to take the spring chill off the air. The moldings and ceiling cornices were as ornate as the furnishings.

Her gaze came back to rest on Jordan, whose own gaze had never left her face.

"You could certainly qualify for the fairy princess," he said, taking her hand in his. He fondled the pink fingertips, and again Bergitta was startled by the effect his slightest touch had on her. She began to feel queasy inside, but it was a delicious queasiness that spread throughout her body. She was completely helpless to resist when he held her head in his hands and caressed her lips with his.

"Goodnight fairy princess," he said, kissing her eyes closed before he departed for his bedroom.

The phone rang while Bergitta was bathing the next morning. She had no intention of listening to Jordan's conversation, but could not help it that his voice carried so clearly from the phone just outside the door.

"Clare!" she heard him say. "How are you?" There was a pause, and Bergitta found herself remembering the eve of the wedding when Clare had called Jordan at his home.

"How did you know where to find me?" he was asking. "Oh, of course. Beryl has a copy of our hotel reservations in case my father becomes ill again." He paused. Incisively, he said, "It's too late for that, Clare. You should have thought of the consequences sooner."

Too late for what? What consequences? Bergitta's head spun dizzily. What was Jordan talking about?

"Of course I care what happens to you, Clare. I always have." Again, there was a pause. "No! I told you, it's too late for that!"

Too late for what? Bergitta moaned inwardly. She

could hear his pen scratching against the message pad. "Yes, I've got the address. Of course you can count on me. Promise you'll do nothing hasty or foolish. It is of the utmost importance that you stay calm and take care of yourself. You'll be hearing from me as soon as I can make arrangements. Goodbye, Clare, darling."

Bergitta squeezed back the tears, angry that it should matter to her that Jordan and Clare still loved each other—but it did—*terribly*!

She waited until he had left the small sitting room that divided the bedrooms of the hotel suite before she left the tub. She dressed in the bridal finery native to the Dutch, her thoughts spinning. How could Jordan be so sincere in his lovemaking if his heart was still with Clare? It didn't make sense. If only he had insisted it was over between them; instead, he had taken her address and phone number and promised to be in touch. *He probably wants to say lovely romantic things to her over the phone when he's alone*, she decided, tears beginning to fall freely.

Libby rang up to say she had a headache and would like to be excused from the day's events; therefore, when Bergitta needed help fastening the miniscule buttons on the back of the dress, she had to go into the next room looking for Jordan. He was nowhere to be found.

When Heiberscham called for them, she told him Jordan had gone on ahead. It was the only plausible explanation she could think of.

At the parade grounds he was nowhere to be seen. Right until the last minute, she waited, hopeful. Surely he had not been serious about his intention to duck out of his responsibilities, however unpleasant he considered them to be.

When time ran out and still Jordan had not appeared, Bergitta was furious. How contemptible of him to disregard protocol totally.

Chris showed up ready to complete the photographic

series for "Budding Love Blossoms," and when she expressed frustration at Jordan's absence, he commented, "I saw him just a few minutes ago at the hotel exchequer. He was telegraphing money to someone and had run into some technical problem transferring the funds. Had something to do with a computer system breakdown."

"Did he say he would be here?" Bergitta asked impatiently.

"He didn't say anything, because he never knew I was there. I had the distinct impression that this was a very confidential thing. In fact, he told the cashier it was a life-and-death matter. I faded into the woodwork before he could see me."

Bergitta couldn't decide who was more disgusting—Chris or Jordan. Of course it had to be Clare he was sending money to, but surely he could have taken care of that after the parade. His absence was inexcusable.

From her lofty position where she stood in the center of one of the two intertwined wedding rings atop the float, she waved at the cheering crowds below. This was the pinnacle, wasn't it? Then why did she feel so empty? Her name was on the front of every fashion cover, or would be on the next issues, so where was the thrill, the joy? Instead there was only the sting of disappointment and loneliness. Success was ashes without someone to share it with. And Jordan wasn't there.

She continued the forced smile and the automatic actions expected of her as the parade's grand marshal and America's official representative to the Dutch tulip festival. Why shouldn't she enjoy this moment alone, she asked herself. After all, she had worked harder and was smarter than anyone else on the design staff. No one had helped her. She had done it herself!

The rings pivoted in a slight breeze as they were designed to do. At the point where they joined to make an arch, a gilded cage with two lovebirds was hanging. They fluttered and began to bill and coo.

113

No, that isn't fair, Bergitta decided. She had not done it alone. She would not have done it at all if Design House had not recognized her ability and given her the opportunity to develop her talent. She would be forever grateful for that. Design House should be represented here today to share in an event that would receive world-wide press coverage. Instead, Jordan had proved himself once again to be the irresponsible playboy. Design House meant nothing to him, even though he was its acting president.

The parade was scheduled to halt midroute while the marching bands performed special numbers. It was then that she saw Jordan making his way through the crowd. Just as the trumpets heralded, he came up the stairway and ascended the pedestal beside her, making the whole thing appear as though it had been planned that way. He pulled a cord, releasing the two lovebirds, who circled their heads while he bent and kissed her beneath the arch of wedding rings. The crowd went wild. So did the pounding of Bergitta's heart. Suddenly everything was right because Jordan was there. She had a sinking feeling that this was how it would be from now on. Jordan seemed to make her life complete. Where had the independent, self-sufficient designer gone? She had surmounted all obstacles to success and then abdicated the throne by allowing her heart to become vulnerable to the man she had married for business reasons only!

When the parade moved on and the lovebirds had returned to their perch in the cage, Jordan turned to her and caught both her hands in his.

"I'm sorry, Bergitta, darling. I had no intention of leaving you stranded like this. An emergency came up that I thought I could take care of before you ever missed me from the hotel room, but I ran into a snag. Please forgive me?"

His eyes were melting the stony coldness that had crept in with his endearment. He had called Clare "dar-

114

ling" also. Did the word mean nothing to him?

If she could believe the look that now held her like a physical embrace, she had nothing to fear from Clare or anyone else. Could she trust him? If she loved him, she must! Her heart would not allow her to do otherwise.

Chapter Eight

Tired, but exhilarated from a long day, Bergitta returned to the hotel room, leaving Jordan to finish the honors at a reception following the tulip festival in the downstairs ballroom of the hotel. She had just finished a relaxing bath and had slid into a pair of comfortable blue jeans when Western Union called. It was a message from New York for Jordan, and assuming that Design House was the sender, Bergitta drew a pad and pencil from the desk drawer. Her hand froze, poised in midair as she listened to the words: *Darling! How good of you to come to my rescue! I received the money, and you saved a life, my lover. Can't wait until this is all over and I can be with you again. My love always, Clare.*

Choking, she told the voice on the telephone to call back later when Mr. Worthington could accept the message himself since it was of a personal nature.

She flung the pencil down and rushed into her bedroom where she steadied herself against the dresser top. She looked into the mirror. *You fool! You utter fool!* she blazed at the reflection of herself. *You got caught up in your own fantasy and began believing it! How stupid can you get?*

Whatever had intervened to stop Clare and Jordan's wedding was clearly only a temporary intervention. Jordan's romantic attentions were obviously only a pleasant diversion to amuse himself until he and Clare could pick up where they left off. She was being used as his toy. No doubt her virtue was a challenge to his cavalier spirit, she seethed.

Bergitta tore around the room, ripping off the jeans and jerking on a dark, unobtrusive suit. She scrambled for suitable accessories, whipped her hair back into its customary knot, searched in her purse for the trusty reading glasses, and was back at the desk five minutes from when she had last left it.

She scribbled a message on the pad: "Jordan. I am meeting with Libby in her room for consultation on the Palace children's design line. We will be out to dinner all evening." She signed her initials with a flourish and propped the note up where he would be sure to see it, then left quickly.

On the way up in the elevator, she regained her composure. When Libby opened the door, Bergitta was even able to feign extreme sympathy for Jordan, who she said needed a restful evening alone. She asked if Libby would like to work for a while with her, discussing fabrics and construction methods for a new design line. Libby unhesitatingly agreed, saying it would be good to "get back in the harness again." When Bergitta arrived back at the suite at one a.m. she was relieved to find Jordan had already retired and no questions would be asked or explanations required.

Jordan was unusually quiet at the breakfast table the next morning. Room service had served it on the terrace overlooking the pool and formal gardens. It was a brilliant morning, but a cloud hung over the couple.

"Do you really think it was wise to raise doubts about our relationship by going off on your own as you did last evening?" Jordan asked, his manner severe. "Heiberscham invited us to his home for dinner. It would have been a wonderful public relations opportunity. He heads up the World Trade Commission. I had already accepted the invitation for both of us, and it was

117

most embarrassing to have to cancel."

"You should never have accepted for both of us. Whatever made you presume you could make my social engagements?"

Jordan buttered a date-nut muffin, looking long and hard at her. "Something is different, Bergitta. A day ago it wouldn't have mattered. Is it the delayed appearance on the float yesterday that still has you in a tiff?"

She shook her head stubbornly. "You imagine things, Jordan. I am not in a tiff and nothing has changed. It's just that I am my own person, and I think you have begun to take the role of husband too seriously. In public we have no other choice but to play the game. In private, let's try to remember who we really are."

Jordan turned the thick mug of coffee around and around in his hands with dexterity. His eyes never left Bergitta as he appeared to be deep in thought.

"Perhaps you're right, Bergitta. Perhaps it *is* time that we remember who we are. I am your employer. As long as you are on an all-expense-paid trip on company business, I will dictate your appearances and schedule as I see fit. Does that clarify our respective roles sufficiently?" His eyes were like flint.

"I think so," she said, tight-lipped. "If you will excuse me now, I have to pack."

"The plane doesn't leave for Switzerland until tomorrow."

"I'm not going on the ski trip with you, Jordan. Since it's not business, I'm sure you will not deny me a few days to myself."

"Wrong!" He uttered an oath. "The trip is very much business. Call it PR if you like, but the Design House bride will accompany her groom at all times. I have no taste for an inquisitive press." He pushed her chair back under the table from where she had scraped it back just a few minutes before.

"Finish your breakfast, Bergitta."

Two days later they were standing on a promontory overlooking the mountains and valleys of the Alps range.

Jordan adjusted the viewfinder on the telescope and held it while Bergitta took her position. "Oh, I see it now!" she squealed. "It's a nest of baby eagles there in the rock formations."

"You got it," he grinned. "Now wasn't that worth getting out of bed for?"

"What can I say?" she grinned back. "I always get out of bed when someone threatens me with a can of shaving cream."

"I'm glad it was effective," he grinned.

"So were Hitler's gestapo tactics," she retorted.

He grew suddenly serious. "Legend has it that this private resort was where he learned to ski as a boy."

She shivered. "I wish you hadn't told me that. He was the cause of so much pain and destruction that I don't like sharing the same roof with his memory."

"He was driven by ambition and the need for power. That often is a combination that brings about destruction—in one's own life, if not in others'."

"Only if taken to an extreme," she reminded him, knowing his double meaning was intended for her because of her dedication to her career.

"Does one ever know where the line is, though, any more than a diver is aware that he has entered a deadly bliss when he refuses to come up from the sea? It gets hold of you."

They had begun walking around the balustraded balcony that circled the ski lodge. Bergitta knew Jordan was impatient with her for having spent all her time at the lodge with her drawing board set up in one corner of their bedroom. She was up until all hours feverishly sketching the new children's line she was ready to submit to Grayson's, Inc. Couturier fashions for children were a coming thing. She had immersed herself in work partly from the innate drive that kept her motor racing and partly to recover from Jordan's sharp rebuke when he had exercised his authority as president of the company.

"Come with me today, Bergitta." He looked at her pensively as she looked over the vastness of the mountains and sky.

"How could he spend his early years in a place this peaceful and still grow up to incite more war and terror?" she mused.

"Who? Hitler?" he gawked at her in surprise. Then he sighed. "I would say it was easy if he brought feminine companionship and was ignored as I've been," he said plaintively.

Bergitta laughed. "I could never have that on my conscience. Okay. I'll go to the slopes with you."

Bergitta screamed, tumbled, pitched, and somersaulted her way down the mountain, while Jordan glided smoothly alongside, yelling out instructions and insisting that she get up on her feet again after each painful confrontation with the snowy ground.

"I think I hate you," she screamed.

He laughed without the slightest trace of guilt. "A few spills are good for you. You're just taking out your frustration on me."

She clambered to her feet, stuck her hands on her hips, and glared at him. "You like to laugh at me, don't you?" she stormed, tears near the surface. "Now that you see I am basically uncoordinated and congenitally afraid of heights, don't you care that I might break a leg, or something?"

"Afraid of heights!" he scoffed. "On this child's slope?" He began to brush the snow from the shoulders and pants of her ski togs. "The most you could do is bruise your backside." He dropped a kiss on her forehead. "I do care about you, Bergitta. I wouldn't want one of your limbs to be broken. They are much too lovely." He kissed her lips, and through lowered eye-

120

lashes she looked into his eyes.

"Oh, Jordan! You confuse me so." She turned and began to ski down the mountain with careful, deliberate motions.

It was late afternoon and all but Bergitta and Jordan were still on the slopes. He had given in to her pleas good-naturedly and had returned to the lodge to sit before the huge stone fireplace sipping a delicious hot mocha.

"What you lack in skill you make up for with pluck," Jordan teased her.

"I don't feel so plucky," Bergitta grumbled. "The word would be *lucky* that I didn't break my neck."

"You have to admit it was fun once you got the hang of it."

Bergitta gave him a wide smile, feeling the pride of accomplishment. Before she had turned in her ski poles she had conquered the basic balance positions and moves.

"Another lesson tomorrow?" he began to trace the design at the neck of the soft white crocheted sweater she wore.

"Mm-hm. If you like."

"I like," he said throatily, his mouth descending to hers.

She moved abruptly and went to stand beside the stone hearth. As she leaned against the mantel, the light from the fire picked up the fiery red lights in her tousled hair, making it rival the brilliance of the sun setting over the white-clad hills.

"What is it, Bergitta? I thought we agreed a long time ago to bury the hatchet and be friends."

"Jordan, I think we must have a different interpretation of what friendship is. I see it as a bond between two people that allows trust to develop. You seem to expect the sensual to develop."

He threw up his hands. "I can't help myself where

you are concerned." He patted the seat beside him on the rustic cowhide couch. "Come sit. I promise to be good as a Boy Scout."

Bergitta crossed the old oak plank floor and sat beside him on the two-seater, drawing up her well-formed legs under her comfortably.

"How is Clare these days?" she asked casually, bending to fasten the loose buckle on her ankle strap so that he could not read the more-than-casual interest in her expression.

"Clare is out of work," he said shortly. "That should tell you how she is." He laughed mirthlessly. "It logically follows that she is out of money. I had to wire her some."

"You still feel responsible for her, don't you," Bergitta said testily.

Jordan glanced at her sharply. "As a matter of fact, I don't. It was a special set of circumstances. In fact, I really sent the money in the interest of another human being who stood to lose without it," he said grimly.

"I just assumed you two would get back together as soon as this marriage had served its purpose."

A hurt expression enveloped him. "Clare and I have nothing between us. I thought you understood that."

Bergitta was puzzled. She supposed the sentiments *could* have been all on Clare's part.

"Does Clare agree that there is nothing between you?"

Jordan was hesitant in answering. "She may have some hope for a future. But there is none," he said definitely. Cognizant of her line of questioning, he asked, "Is that what's been bothering you, Bergitta?" He caught her in his arms. "Surely you don't think—I guess you do," he sighed, seeing the guarded look in her eyes and the tension in her body.

"Let's just let it go for now, Jordan," she said quietly. "Let's concentrate on a lovely relationship that we will call friendship."

122

Just then, they were interrupted by two of Jordan's old skiing buddies, Dan and Rolf and their wives, Erica and Pamela. There was a lot of laughter and camaraderie among the three men who had been partners in a real estate deal several years ago and had kept the friendship alive with their annual ski jaunts to the Alps. The ski lodge had been part of the large land acquisition, and they had decided to keep it in joint ownership for just this use.

The couples were delighted at Jordan's marriage and immediately accepted Bergitta as part of their company. They chattered excitedly about their business ventures and about their children. Something stirred in Bergitta that evening at the table romanticized by candles in wine bottles. The good-natured banter, the half-serious arguments between spouses, their concerns about the future for their children, and in Dan and Pamela's case, plans for a new home left Bergitta feeling cheated.

"Where are you and Jordan going to live after the honeymoon?" Pamela asked.

Bergitta was startled by the question and started to explain that they had not gotten that far with their plans, but Jordan, perceiving her awkwardness leapt in and explained that they would live at his penthouse while they shopped for a house on the island.

The conversation went on to something else, but Bergitta found herself once again living the dream. These were the rich ones. Their lives were rich with living, loving, and having each other. Their gold would be the golden years spent together under a colorful arch of both happy and poignant memories.

After dinner the six played Trivial Pursuit until the early hours of the morning when Erica and Rolf finally won.

In her room, Bergitta dressed for bed in a feminine, lacy pink flannel nightgown to protect her from the coldness of the lodge bedroom. Jordan tactfully kept company with his friends, as he had done every night to allow her privacy. Usually he came in and retired on the couch long after she was asleep. Tonight, he came in earlier.

"They're really some bunch, aren't they?" he said appreciatively.

"Yes, they are," she sleepily agreed. "I can see why you keep coming back here for a reunion. It's restful and they're fun to be with."

"I'm glad you see it that way," he nodded. "We all agreed to go on a safari together, as soon as the last of the publicity shots are taken in Rome."

Bergitta sat straight up in bed. "Jordan, you didn't!"

Seeing her dismay, he rejoined mildly, "Why not? You just said you enjoyed being with them."

"I don't enjoy shooting wild game, though!"

"Maybe you'll be better at it than you are at skiing," he said, smiling sardonically.

Before she had time to think, she had flung the book she was reading at Jordan. It sailed across the room, landing with a heavy thud against the side of his head. He dropped to the floor.

In a flash she was beside him, taking his head in her hands to inspect for damage.

He moaned heavily. In her consternation she failed to catch the theatrics of his tone, allowing him full advantage of the situation. His arms closed around her like a steel vise, and he pulled her to the floor beside him. "I know a wild game that's sure to be exciting," he said coaxingly as he nuzzled her neck and dropped kisses along her throbbing pulses.

A feminine voice called from the hallway. "Hey, you two! Is everything all right in there? I thought I heard someone fall."

Bergitta gathered her matching robe and her dignity to her and sped through French doors to the balcony which connected to their bedroom.

Jordan jerked the hallway door open. "Don't you

know better than to do that to a couple of honeymooners?" he barked.

Erica blushed and backed away with muttered apologies.

Bergitta turned as Jordan came toward her on the balcony. She backed off. "You've turned into a wolf, Jordan! I think it must be the full moon," she laughed, still backing away.

He imitated a low growl. "A full moon always sends the wolf howling after the fox." She succumbed to his questing lips as they trapped their prey.

The young couple stood locked in their kiss as the full moon rose higher over the tallest mountain, half peeking, half smiling at the two lost in its spell. A translucent glow enveloped them as it did the snowy peaks and surrounding valleys.

Bergitta drew away from his intoxicating charms and dreamily gazed around her. "This is an enchanted place," she murmured.

He tasted her lips again, leaving a misty fragrance like a heady wine. She leaned against him, drinking in his male essence.

"I called the office this afternoon," he said. "According to Bernie, nothing has landed on our desks more urgent than concluding our honeymoon on a safari. And who knows?" he mused. "All kinds of magic happen in Africa."

"There you go, arranging my life again," she teased.

"Correction. *Our* life."

He sounded so convincing, Bergitta gasped. *Did* he mean it? She looked at him. His expression was as sincere as though the unusual circumstances of their marriage had never existed.

Her heart began to beat in her throat. Was she ready to meet his demands? She gulped. Her own emotions were tangled in knots where he was concerned!

He bent and kissed her passionately, in a way that she felt clear down to her toes. He had her under his spell.

A door blammed open and allowed raucous laughter to float up to the balcony where they stood.

Dan cupped his hands around his mouth and called up to them. "The moonshine is as bright as daylight. We've decided to do some night skiing. Want to come?"

Jordan's eyes burned into hers, challenging the very stronghold of her resistance. "I'll let you decide, Bergitta. Shall we go inside, or shall we join the others on the slopes?"

Bergitta knew it was a momentous decision. If it were the wrong one, there would be no turning back.

She steeled herself against the strong thighs that crushed their weight against hers and the broad chest that was like a protective wall. She looked into his eyes, pleading for his understanding.

"I choose to go skiing with you, Jordan."

The next day as they were leaving the small but thriving Swiss village on their way to the fashion capital of the world, Paris, Jordan stopped at a bank in town to exchange some currency.

"Isn't that Chris?" Bergitta pointed to a thin blond-haired man leaning against one of the pillars in front of the bank.

Jordan seemed startled, too. He had not advised anyone of his whereabouts except his father. Beryl, of course, was responsible.

Chris hailed him down as he and Bergitta approached. "I have a message for you," Chris said, looking uneasily at Bergitta as though he would like for her to disappear.

"Shoot!" Jordan put his arm around Bergitta. "My wife can hear anything you have to say."

Still he hesitated. Bergitta excused herself and started to move on, but Jordan clamped his arm tighter about her.

Chris shifted his weight from one foot to the other and stroked his mustache. "Clare called the hotel looking for you. She said she needs more money."

Bergitta felt the arm around her turn to stone. She flickered a glance at Jordan. His eyes were steely hard, but his voice was smooth as he answered, "How very clever of Clare to remember you were there to convey messages."

"Yeah." His lower lip dangled loosely. "She must have been desperate."

"Or frightened," Jordan said, his words as sharp as the cutting edge of a blade. Bergitta had the distinct impression there was an innuendo in them.

She and Jordan went on into the bank. As Jordan went to the mail express window, she watched him incredulously. He was sending her money! *So much for the "just good friends" alibi*, she thought forlornly.

She was angry. How dare he try to seduce her into loving him when he obviously was still involved with his ex-fiancée?

On the way to the airport in the little rented car, he watched her from the corner of his eye. "I knew you'd get mad," he said accusingly, as though she were the one who had done something wrong.

She swallowed a retort. She refused to be drawn into this.

He stopped the car at a scenic overlook and got out. "We have some time," he said. He came around to help her from the car.

They stood on the precipice that overlooked the snowy mountains and valleys sun-washed with gold. The stunning magnificence of the scene was overwhelming!

He reached for her hand and began to massage it gently while he perused her face, now shadowed with the gloom of disappointment.

"Bergitta," he said softly, "look at the vastness of this space. Millions of years ago it was formed and hangs on nothing that we can see, yet we trust our very existence to it. Sometimes we have to trust each other in that same way—when there are no reasonable explanations and belief seems unmerited. I need your trust. There is no relationship between Clare and me other than my decent concern for another human being. I want you to believe that." He held her hand to his face while his deep, searching gaze held her eyes.

"Why do you want my trust, Jordan? Why is it so important?" she asked in a barely audible voice.

"Because..." he hesitated as though on the verge of committing himself to her, then said, "because *our* relationship is the most important thing in my life. We have something special that needs a chance to develop. I don't think it can without complete trust."

"Don't you think that's asking a bit much?" She lifted thick curving lashes to him. "After all, it was only a month ago that you were engaged to Clare. How could you say so soon that there is nothing left?"

"Because there was nothing to begin with," he said emphatically. "I know that because I felt nothing but indifference and relief when the wedding plans changed. At first I was concerned for her physical welfare, but once I knew she was safe, I felt a tremendous release."

"It sounds like—"

"It sounds like human concern," he interrupted her.

Her emerald eyes sparkled with the brilliance of unshed tears. "I wish I knew your sincerity to be the truth, Jordan."

"You can accept it as the truth," he urged her. "That would be trust. The decision is yours, Bergitta."

She considered his words carefully. His firm, unrelenting jaw gave no choice except for trust. He was being totally honest with her, she knew. She could tell it by his dead-set determination.

"All right, Jordan," she smiled. "I trust what you tell me to be the truth. If you say there is nothing between you and Clare, I believe you. I just didn't want to make myself vulnerable if you two had had a lovers' quarrel and were planning a rendezvous at the first opportunity."

"That isn't going to happen. You can believe me."

"I do," she said, raising limpid eyes to his.

The flight back to England was smooth, and by evening they were reunited with the *Ocean Queen* and the yacht's crew who would take them down the coast, stopping at ports along the way for more photographs before the couple flew onto Rome.

Libby was already on board, but Chris had not yet made it. Reluctantly Jordan consented to an overnight berth, threatening to leave without the photographer if he did not report by ten the next morning.

That night the crew threw a party for the returning bride and bridegroom and regaled them with stories of their jaunt around the northern tip of Ireland where they had taken a group of Arab investors looking for land acquisitions. These chartered trips were the bread and butter of the *Ocean Queen* and financially justified its existence in the company.

Chris barely made it the next morning and received only scowls for a welcome, with a curt, "I'll see you in my quarters in an hour," from Jordan.

When Bergitta thought enough time had elapsed for the confrontation to be over, she went to her cabin. But a strong argument was still in progress.

"But you don't know for sure—do you?" she heard Chris sneer.

"I don't know for sure, but if I ever find out that you have been hurting Clare—" Jordan's tone was menacing and ended in a low growl.

Bergitta leaned her back against the door jamb. Her knees buckled under her. There it was again! Jordan's intense concern for Clare was beyond understanding. It was hard to believe he could be so protective of her without being in love with her! She squeezed her eyes tight and remembered the sincerity of his countenance that day as they had stood overlooking the mountain view. It was a look that said he could be trusted to the ends of the earth. He had even reminded her that she had made a contract of trust with him from the very beginning, and he had asked her to honor that contract by trusting him not ever to do anything to hurt her. She gritted her teeth. Could she do it? Was she able to dismiss the intimate telephone conversation between him and Clare? Could she forget the anguish in his voice when he told her not to do anything foolish?

Chris stormed into the passage and saw her. "I suppose you're snooping on me, too?" he inquired disdainfully.

"I don't know what you're talking about," she said coolly. "I assumed you were getting a justly deserved reprimand for delaying the voyage."

"So that's what you thought! Well, you've got a lot to learn about your husband! I'd say in only a matter of weeks you'll find out what's in store for you." He laughed evilly and turned on his heel.

Bergitta willed her knees to be steady as she walked into the quarters she and Jordan shared. He stood at the large plate-glass doors, arms folded over his chest, looking thunderously at the sea.

"Bad scene?" she inquired lightly.

He shrugged indifferently, his back as rigid as granite.

"You were pretty rough on him."

"Not nearly as rough as he deserved," Jordan said through tightly drawn lips.

If Bergitta had hoped for an explanation after she revealed she had heard part of the conversation, she was disappointed. Jordan was indifferent to anything except that her presence in the room had improved his disposition. "I'll look at the designs you wanted me to see," he offered.

She was hardly in the frame of mind to share the sketches she and Libby had collaborated on, but she drew out the portfolio of children's fashions anyway.

Jordan scrutinized them carefully. After he had leafed through the sketches a second time, he said with acute directness, "They're not exactly your Shirley Temple look, are they?"

Sensing his keen disapproval, she spurted caustically, "I hope not! I think I'm more imaginative that that."

He frowned. "They seem little more than copies of what their mothers might wear."

"Exactly. But with a touch of naiveté in the details, such as the bow on the off-shoulder number." She used her pencil to point out the childlike touches on the sophisticated designs. She nibbled the eraser on her pencil, as an idea began to form. "What do you think about resurrecting the mother-daughter, look-alike fashions? This time, instead of putting ruffles and lace on mother's costume, we would reverse the concept and put a little sophistication into the daughter fashions. It would be a new concept for Design House."

Jordan followed her words carefully. "I don't know— would it sell? What is the market psychology on it?"

"I'm not sure. The current mood is to rejuvenate the styles of forty years ago. The mother-daughter, look-alike theme would fit into that reference. Whether or not the market is ready for some innovative changes on the theme is another question."

Jordan understood thoroughly, as he indicated with a nod. "The half-child, half-woman idea might best be left to the teenage line," he commented, perusing the sketches one more time. "They're glamorous, but I'm just not convinced the designs have enough integrity to sell."

"If they have the *Bergitta* label they'll sell!" she said more curtly than she intended.

He laid the sketches aside and studied her just as carefully as he had the design work.

"Design House has never had to bypass good design and lean on past laurels to sell a product," he said coolly. "I think you know our philosophy is to market honest design and superior workmanship."

His rebuke stung. She felt tears spring to her eyes and

quickly averted them. He just as quickly turned her back to face him, cradling her chin in one hand. "Use your credible, hard-earned name to influence fashion trends for the better. You have a real opportunity to make a valid impact on the industry."

Bergitta sniffled and nodded. "I accept that, Jordan. In the giddy daze of success, I guess I lost my balance. The designs *are* contrived. I'm sorry."

Jordan swept her into his arms and occupied himself flicking away the tears that glistened on the deep amber, curved lashes that veiled the clear pools of green.

"You're really rough on a guy, you know it?" he said gruffly. "A real hit in the head!"

She swept her eyelashes upward in sensual surprise. "All I did was say 'I'm sorry.' "

"That's all!" he mimicked. "That's all it takes to rip my heart out by the roots."

She sighed and wiped her eyes. "What has happened to my toughness? I thought I had my professional armor permanently in place. I haven't cried in years!"

"Somehow, I'm rather glad it slipped out of place. It's good to know that a sensitive heart beats underneath."

Bergitta fell silent. Jordan had just hit on the truth. It was a sensitive heart that made her care about Jordan's opinion of her work. He had to matter a lot in her life for her to care in a personal way what he thought of her work.

They had lunch in their suite, and afterward Jordan insisted she pick up her pencil and search for fresh ideas. He sat near her with a book and smiled encouragingly from time to time.

By late afternoon a soft rain was falling. Jordan stretched and yawned, then came over to glance at the sketches. "Hmmm," he murmured, studying them and dropping them one by one into a stack. "I like." He pointed out one in particular.

Bergitta smiled. "This is an adaptation of the dress my mother made for my kindergarten graduation."

"I knew there was a reason why I like it," Jordan grinned. "I can just see you as a little girl flirting with the best-looking little boy in class."

A musical chortle of admission fell from Bergitta's lips.

He pulled her up from the drawing board and drew her to the couch. "You deserve a rest after an afternoon of hard labor," he told her.

"You can say that again. After chipping away for new ideas, I feel like my head is full of rock fragments!"

"In that case, I have the right treatment." He turned her back toward him and began to massage the tightened muscles at the base of her neck. She nestled back against the solid wall of his chest and visibly began to relax.

"Ohhh, this *is* a treat," she crooned in ecstasy.

Jordan drew in his breath. "For all your sophistication, you still are an adorable child," he murmured beneath lips that had begun to explore the soft curve in the slender column of her neck.

His earthy, masculine scent was intoxicating. She felt herself succumbing to the pleasurable assault he was making on her senses. He slipped his arms down to encircle her waist and pulled her tightly against him while his lips roved her silken tresses.

Struggling for control over the tide of desire that swept her, she pushed her palms against his hard thighs behind her. The light from her drawing board was like a saving beacon. She eased out of his arms. "I really think I could finish that last sketch before dinner if I tried," she said.

Frustrated, Jordan watched her cross the room. "And then what? Are you going to send it to London via a porpoise postman? There's no rush on your designs, Bergitta."

She leveled her gaze at him. "And there's no rush on yours, either, Jordan," she said quietly.

"Ouch!" he winced. "You really know how to hurt a

guy." Undaunted, he ambled over to the drawing board where she was perched and swiveled the tall stool around to face him. He bent over so that his lips were poised above hers, and slowly he teased them with his light touches.

With bated breath, she waited for his full kiss and leaned forward in eager response. His lips moved against hers and felt them grow soft and pliable beneath his rousing demands. In a voice roughened by emotion, he said, "That drawing board is merely a barrier you put between us because you don't trust yourself any more than you trust me!" He kissed her again, fully.

Her moan ended in a soft whimper. "I confess. I'm just a lump of mindless putty in your hands."

He looked up and saw the dangerous gleam in her eye that belied her words. He grimaced. "As far as your vulnerability to me is concerned, you resemble putty about as much as a pillar of concrete does," he scoffed, lifting her up by her elbows. This time he concluded the conversation by announcing, "Time to dress for dinner."

Chapter Nine

Chris Jamison took a quick succession of shots while Bergitta balanced on the curb of the great Trevi fountain, barefoot and carefree. However, the effort to keep her precarious balance and the stone beneath her feet left her anything but carefree.

Patiently she went through the poses necessary for the "Rome-ing the Ruins" sequence. They had spent most of the day going the rounds of the Pantheon, the Arch of Constantine, and the Colosseum. Every scene required a change of costume, each a breathtaking concoction for the well-dressed tourist bride.

Chris had been relentless in his quest for perfection, sometimes humoring her into the desired attitude and expression, sometimes demanding that she discipline her performance. Bergitta was ready to drop in her tracks when Jordan finally called a halt to the rigorous work.

On the way to the hotel in a cab, she weakly commented that never again would she take for granted the energy and expertise required of a professional model. She then sank into a tired stupor from which she did not rouse until Jordan half dragged her from the cab, supporting her with his arm around her back until they reached the room.

He ran a tub of hot bath water, but when he found

her sound asleep on the bed, he did not disturb her, even though dusk had not yet fallen.

Three hours later she came from the bathroom pink and fresh and dewy from her bath. Knotting the tie on her pink velour robe, she proclaimed, "I feel like a new person."

"You look like one. A few hours ago I had serious thoughts of taking you to the emergency room for treatment of exhaustion."

She realized he was deadly serious. "If you knew it had come to that point, why didn't you stop Chris before you did?"

"Because when you went, it was all of a sudden. You turned that lovely ashen gray the same as your bonnet in the gray pinstripe number."

He glanced at his watch. "In the summer, opera is presented at the ruins of the Baths of Caracalla. It's something spectacular to see if you're feeling up to it."

"I'd love to go," Bergitta smiled shyly, touched by his thoughtfulness. Her creamy complexion glowed translucent under the soft light of the Victorian lamp. A muscle twitched in Jordan's jaw.

"You'd better go get dressed now before I find something better to do with our evening."

Taking his warning seriously, Bergitta hastened to change into the lime and aqua creation that fell in easy folds about her sylph's figure. She brushed her hair loose, and with a few flicks of the brush, she achieved a blousy style that she knew Jordan liked.

From his darkly glowing eyes she could tell Jordan was pleased with how she looked. In his open admiration, he almost forgot the moment required something of him.

"I have a present for you." He held out a small, silver-wrapped box tied with a floret of ribbons.

Delighted, she picked the ribbon apart with delicate pink-tipped fingers. "What's the occasion? Did I forget my birthday or something?" she said, struck with sudden conscience.

"No," he laughed. Then he said, "When I saw these, I thought of you."

The jewelry box sprang open under her touch, and she gasped aloud. A necklace of blue opals surrounded by cut diamonds nested there; beside them was a matching pair of earrings.

"They're the most beautiful things I've ever seen in my life," she whispered reverently, lifting the white gold chain in her fingers. "I can't accept them, of course. They're much too expensive."

She looked up to see a dark cloud of hurt hovering over Jordan. "I'm not buying your favors if that's what you are worried about," he said hoarsely. "There are no strings attached."

"I'm sorry, Jordan. I didn't mean to be ungrateful. It's just that I have never been given anything this exquisite before."

"Then that makes it all the more special to me," he said with satisfaction. He began to remove the necklace from the box and placed it around her throat. Her fingers clutched it passionately.

"But why, Jordan? Why would you give me a gift like this?" Her gaze searched his face wonderingly. She saw him swallow to gain control of his voice.

"Do you really not know, Bergitta?" he asked throatily, his deep searching gaze joining hers. "Do you really not know?" He bent and kissed her on the lips.

"If it makes you feel better, just consider it a bonus from the boss who appreciates the long hard hours you have put in."

The Baths of Caracalla were magnificent. The huge rectangular pools that had once been the public baths of Rome were flanked by colorful gardens. There were abstract-patterned floor mosaics surrounding the pools. Jordan watched Bergitta's enjoyment with delight.

137

Her delicate features and patrician bearing seemed to fit here among the carved classics of the past. Her face was an expressive mosaic of her many feelings.

"It's all so lovely—so very beautiful," she breathed as they wandered the grounds after the opera.

"It would have to be, to provide a setting worthy of you," he said with quiet feeling. "Your beauty outshines it all."

She turned to him, and seeing the calm adoration, she gulped, "Thank you, Jordan." Her answering smile said it all.

The evening ended all too soon. Bergitta didn't want to leave this wonderland where the tall cedars touched the stars with their proud spires and then fell into the reflecting pool.

"Let's stay all night, Jordan," she laughed impulsively, like a child.

"I'd stay anywhere all night with you, my dear Bergitta. It could only be enchanting." He lifted her hand to his lips.

"Thank you again for the lovely opals and diamonds. I don't deserve them, you know."

"I don't give gifts because people deserve them. I gave you these because it gives me pleasure. I hope they will give you pleasure, also."

"Oh, Jordan. They do—they have—they always will!" she breathed fervently. Tears gathered in the corners of her eyes. "Oh dear! There I go turning on the waterworks again. What's wrong with me, I wonder?"

He looked at her with a speculative smile. "I wonder," he repeated softly.

Paris, the city of romance! Bergitta inhaled its sweet spring fragrance and knew she would never get enough of it. They were in a horse-drawn carriage; it was evening; and the everpresent Chris was everywhere taking pictures—front, side, and center. After they had covered the most famous gardens and squares along the Av-

138

enue des Champs Elysées, the Eiffel Tower, and the Arc de Triomphe, Jordan terminated the session so that he could show Bergitta his own private Paris.

After freshening up at the hotel, they took a cab down the Boulevard Michel which ran from the Seine south through the Latin Quarter. This was a district inhabited mostly by students and given its name in medieval times when university lectures were given in Latin.

"There are some great cabarets there where you can see an authentic slice of contemporary French culture," Jordan advised her.

Bergitta looked doubtfully at her black silk balloon pants that were gathered onto the cuffs at the knees. She wore a white satin blouse, sheer black stockings, and narrow-heeled black patent pumps. "I hope what I'm wearing will be appropriate."

Jordan chuckled. "*Anything* would be appropriate in these places. You'll see everything from Bohemian makeovers to couturier designs from the most fashionable salons."

They had entered a nightlife arena of flashing neon lights, street bands, and colorfully dressed parties of people swinging along arm in arm, laughing and chattering as they went from one cabaret to the next. Jordan steered her to a sidewalk café where they ate a variety of crepes under a red-striped awning. After their evening meal they lounged in their wrought-iron chairs enjoying a cup of cappucino and clapping to the tunes as people danced in the street. From one passing street vendor Jordan bought a spray of small orchids for her hair; from another, balloons. Bergitta was exploding with laughter. "You know how to make everything fun!" Hand in hand they strolled down the lamplit streets soaking up the carnival atmosphere.

Bergitta was sad when it was time to go back to their hotel suite. Surprisingly, their rooms were contemporary deco in a city that dotes on the French provincial period. The change was welcome.

Bergitta was toweling her hair dry when she joined Jordan in the central living area of their suite. She wrapped the towel around her head forming a pink terry turban that matched her velour robe.

"I confirmed all our appointments with the three fashion houses today," she informed him. "They're all having private showings for us."

Jordan looked up from the newspaper he had been reading.

"I forgot to tell you. I have to make a trip back to New York for a couple of days. There are some documents that need my signature, and I want to check on Pop before I go on the safari."

"Then it will be just Chris, Libby, and me?" she gulped, feeling a painful throb of disappointment.

"I'm sending Libby back to the States. Design House is swamped with orders and needs her. Since the photographing sessions are over, there's no need for Chris to stay either. He can return with the yacht. It's berthed about a hundred miles from here in a port on the English channel.

"Couldn't he stay?" Bergitta pleaded, not yet recovered from the shock that Jordan was leaving. "It will be difficult to get around in the city by myself since I don't speak the language."

"I'll only be gone a couple of days," Jordan snapped, obviously annoyed by her request.

There it was again. His hostility toward Chris was almost tangible.

"Besides," he continued in a calmer vein, "all of the cabbies speak English, and the fashion houses will have interpreters at your disposal."

Seeing her forlorn look, he drew her to the couch with him and cupped her face in his hands. "Do you think I *want* to go off and leave you? I'll miss you like my own life," he declared.

"Then take me with you," she said impulsively.

He shook his head regretfully. "It really is important

for Design House to establish communication with these three particular salons here in Paris. You may interest them in marketing some of our lines." He brought a dossier and went over it with her for a few minutes to acquaint her with the goals he wanted her to accomplish on the visit.

Finished, she laid the folder on the glass and gold coffee table and leaned back against the white linen couch. "When are you leaving?"

"Tomorrow morning. I'll be back by Friday in time for our flight to Lubumbashi where we start the first leg of our safari."

"You'll be gone almost four days, then," Bergitta mused.

"Two days in New York plus travel time," he nodded. "I'm really sorry but it *is* necessary."

"I understand, of course," Bergitta struggled to control the tremor in her voice. If she were in Jordan's place, she would make the same decision. A business cannot be left for weeks, especially with the proprietor suffering ill health as J. W. was. Why, then, was it throwing her so?

"I'm glad you're going to miss me," Jordan drew her close under his arm and cuddled her like a child.

"I didn't say I was going to," she tossed her head. "I plan to spend a *lot* of your money on one of the fanciest safari outfits I can find!"

He leaned back his head and roared. "You do that! To my knowledge the design world hasn't discovered safari wear yet, so I doubt you'll find anything except frumpy khaki," he teased.

She wrinkled her nose. "Ugh. I don't look good at all in frumpy khaki!"

He wrapped her in his arms and contradicted her. "You look good in anything at all."

She raised her lips to meet his gentle command.

Bergitta came in tired after the third day of making

141

the rounds of the small fashion salons. She had been graciously entertained at lunch and dinner on every occasion, but it had been a strain to keep up with the conversation. She determined never again to be caught short of the skills she needed. When she returned to the States she would take some foreign language courses.

She flung her mauve jacket on the sofa and went to answer the phone which was ringing when she came through the door. It was Grayson Thatcher letting her know that three of the four designs she had sent him were being accepted by the princess for her small daughter. Bergitta was elated. There were further instructions, and she began to make notes on a pad beside the telephone. The princess wanted several play fashions cut from the same design, but using hand-loomed fabrics from an economically deprived country. It was the crown's way of expressing goodwill and hopefully stimulating trade by other nations with the backward countries.

What a challenge! Bergitta thought as she hung up the phone. She whirled around the room in delight, then fell on the sofa laughing with pleasure at her success. Who would have thought that the little girl from Iowa would have anything to offer the royal family in Buckingham Palace?

Suddenly she couldn't wait to share the news with Jordan. He was due back tomorrow evening, but she couldn't wait that long. She glanced at her watch. She had been entertained at dinner early. It was only nine o'clock. Since it was six hours earlier in New York, the office should still be open. She could call now.

"Mr. Worthington isn't here. He left the office early," Mindy, the receptionist, informed her.

Bergitta asked to speak to Bernie. After expressing her joy at Bergitta's surprise call, the assistant said, "I don't know where Jordan is. But I know he's had this place jumping ever since he arrived."

Bergitta could hear the scowl in her voice. She

142

cheered up considerably upon learning that one of the salons Bergitta had visited wanted an exclusive contract for their newest line on the European side. Bernie was thrilled, too, to learn that Bergitta's work had been accepted by the princess. Her suggestion that this might lead to further designing for the princess herself was a thought that had already occurred to the young designer.

She was about to conclude the conversation when Bernie asked, "By the way, did you know Clare is back in New York? She's staying with J. W. and Beryl. No one has seen her, though, and rumor has it she's still not accepting modeling work."

Bergitta hung up the phone slowly, lost in thought. Jordan was staying at J. W.'s also, having explained that it would be easier than reopening his apartment. Was Clare the reason he had chosen this particular time to return to New York? Fury welled up in her. She stripped off her clothing and stood under a splintering cold shower, thinking only dark thoughts about Jordan and Clare.

She had already gone to bed and was sound asleep when the phone rang.

"Hello, darling. Sorry I missed your call. Bernie reached me here at J. W.'s."

"Oh, it really wasn't important," she said coolly. "I gave Bernie the message. One of the salons wants an exclusive on our line of playwear, and I thought you might want to get the paperwork started."

"No problem. I have to stay a couple of days longer than I intended, so I can probably bring a contract with me when I return."

Bergitta's heart plummeted. Was he staying because of Clare?

Softly he asked, "Do you miss me as much as I do you?"

"I haven't had time," she lied. In fact, she had gone around with an empty ache ever since he left.

"Oh? Who's taking up your time?"

"As a matter of fact, I've met a couple of people who seem determined to show me every street in Paris." This was not a lie.

There was a pause as Jordan tried to decide whether or not she was serious.

"Well, I'll see you in a few days. Someone from the office will call to let you know the exact time."

Once more Bergitta hung up the phone. She tossed on her side, reassured by his call in one way, but frustrated in another. At least he cared enough to return her call and to say he had missed her. But he had given no reason for the delay of his return. Unfortunately it didn't take much imagination to guess the cause of the delay.

It was a week before he returned, and Bergitta was sure he would give up the idea of going on the safari since they were several days late and the party had already left. But Jordan had made arrangements to take a Jeep and join the safari en route at a certain way station.

At the car rental in Lubumbashi, all but one Jeep had been assigned out. The attendant commented how lucky they were to get the last one. Bergitta grimaced, thinking it a dubious blessing. They had flown from France into the African interior, and already the heat was rising in steamy vapors from the ground.

"We should be there by darkfall, as they say in the wilderness," Jordan grinned, whistling as merrily as a boy gone fishing on a school day.

He had caught her up to date on the business at Design House. Some of the orders had called for unavailable options, and suppliers had to be contacted to work out details. A special board meeting had been called for some particular decisions on which Jordan had wanted their input.

"Everything is under control," he announced happily as they set out in the jungle. "You're a celebrity," he grinned, glancing over at her. "The *New York Times* and *Women's Wear Daily* claim the show had more 'splendor' than any in history. They'll probably hold a ticker-tape parade for you when we get back," he teased.

She blushed at his compliment and wondered why he affected her this way.

She looked around her. Central Africa wasn't towering banana trees and thick vines as she had expected. Instead there were vast expanses of tall grass with occasional clumps and thickets of trees.

The Jeep sputtered and coughed a little bit as they entered a deep forest about lunch time. "Probably overheated," Jordan grunted. "We'll have our picnic now, and then I'll put some water in the radiator."

Bergitta assented and spread out the simple picnic lunch on an old, flat tree stump. They ate quickly, without much conversation, and climbed back into the cooled-off Jeep.

They went deeper and deeper into the interior. It became darker and darker, from both the thicker foliage and the fact that the sun was going down. Jordan pushed on the accelerator and forged on through the ruts of the half-overgrown road.

"Are you sure you took the right turn back there?" Bergitta asked anxiously.

"Of course," he said in a jocular manner. "I don't make wrong turns!"

"Ha! You made a wrong one when you insisted on bringing me along on this—this untamed soirée. I wish I could go back."

"Never go back, Bergitta. Always go forward. *Charge!*" he yelled in a fit of good humor.

The Jeep sputtered to a halt.

Bergitta smirked with satisfaction.

Jordan threw her an aggrieved look and heaved his body over the side of the Jeep to take a look at the engine. He tinkered and tapped and played with the starter in alternate shifts, all to no avail.

"What? You have no mechanical skills tucked away somewhere in all that vast knowledge of the world?" she quipped.

He wiped black grease from his hand onto a towel. "A magician I am not," he declared with chagrin.

Suddenly becoming a realist, Bergitta exclaimed, "Jordan! What are we going to do? We can't spend the night here in the Jeep. The wild animals come out hunting for their prey at night," she shivered.

"That's right!" he affirmed with no qualms about further agitating her. "It's the law of the jungle—survival of the fittest." He grinned. "If a jungle cat were to leap on you, I'd put my money on you any day, judging from the fierceness in your eyes."

"Don't joke!" she snapped. "You got us into this mess, and now you can jolly well get us out of it!"

"I don't know about jolly, but I certainly do plan to get us out. Come on. We'll walk. There's sure to be a village somewhere nearby."

Her eyes grew wide. "I'm not leaving this Jeep."

"Suit yourself," he said, beginning to be impatient. "I'll go."

"No!" Now paralyzed with fear, she clutched his hand.

A rustle in the underbrush startled them. Jordan swiftly reached for his rifle in the back seat. A spear was thrust through the foliage, and the small face of a white African hunter appeared.

Bergitta shrieked as the twisted form of a boy writhed from the leafy shelter and made contorted leaps to the side of the Jeep.

Stunned, they watched the deformed figure.

He thumped his chest. "Hello, I am Zhan-ta!" He smiled broadly.

"Hello, Zhan-ta." Jordan returned his smile. Somehow he made the boy understand their predicament. His eyes sparkled with excitement, and with a signal

146

forward, he led them on a long walk to a clearing. There appeared to be several acres of land where a missionary camp had been set up. Judging from the number of dormitories set up around the camp, the church in the center, a first-aid building, a cafeteria, and another hut of undetermined purpose, Jordan supposed it to be an orphanage operated by a church organization.

The boy half-limped, half-dragged his body across the clearing.

"I think he's taking us to his leader," Jordan said in a theatrical whisper.

Bergitta giggled hysterically. "Just so they're not the 'one-eyed, one-horned, flying purple people-eaters.' "

The boy turned and grinned widely. "We are not cannibals," he said. "We are Christian. Dr. Dan teaches us that way."

Just then a man wearing cut-off jeans and little else emerged from the church where Zhan seemed to be leading them. He folded his deeply tanned arms across his hairy chest and said, "Who are these friends you have brought to us, Zhan?"

There was a twinkle in his eye as Jordan explained their fate.

"Ah, yes." Dr. Dan stroked his beard. "It's not unusual for us to get a few lost souls wandering in from safaris. One of the main trails is near here, and invariably some with no instinct for direction stumble in like lost lambs."

"In our case it's a stalled Jeep. I don't suppose there's any point in asking if there are facilities nearby for repairs."

Dr. Dan seemed to find this highly amusing. "You are five hundred miles into the interior. The road you traveled is not passable most of the year. A supply plane flies in once a week with food and mail. Your best bet is to fly back out with the pilot in his two-seater and bring back the part you need to fix the Jeep. Meanwhile, you're welcome to share what we have in the way of shelter and food."

Bergitta looked around her hesitantly. "When will the supply plane be here?"

"Ah—unfortunately, he just flew out today. It will be a week before he returns. I can offer you lodging until then, but unfortunately you will not be together. We have a women's and a men's dormitory. I live in the men's dormitory, also," he told Jordan.

Jordan had his own room, but Bergitta shared a room with Mara, a young white African who very happily said she was to be married in a matter of days. She was Zhan-ta's sister.

They had not brought their suitcases from the Jeep, so Mara provided Bergitta with a simple white night-dress.

"It is for my wedding night, but you must wear it now. It is the only nice thing I have to offer."

"Oh, no! I couldn't do that, Mara," she said to the dark-haired, tanned woman with shining brown eyes. "You must keep it for your own special night."

"A nightdress does not makes the wedding night," she blushed and smiled shyly. "The love of my husband is what I shall wear."

Bergitta almost envied the love light that shone from her pretty countenance. This was what marriage was supposed to be.

"Who is the young man you are marrying?" Bergitta asked, judging the girl to be barely in her teens herself.

"His name is Wani. He is in training here at the compound to minister the gospel to his own people. After he graduates next week, we will be married and go to pastor a small church we will build."

"That's lovely, Mara. I'm so glad for you. I hope you have a happy life together."

"I know we shall. You see, we not only have our love for each other; we also have the love of the Lord to ce-

148

ment our commitment. That makes our marriage special."

"Yes, it does," Bergitta said musingly, listening to the confidence in Mara's voice.

She thought of her relationship with Jordan and their marriage under false pretenses. It seemed such a travesty of trust when measured by the purity of purpose that Mara and Wani shared.

After a shower taken in a crude, wooden stall, Bergitta fell on the bed too exhausted to sleep. The events of the last few hours had a nightmarish quality about them. Twenty-four hours ago she had been a guest in a sumptuous hotel in Paris. Tonight, after a long flight and a ten-hour ride by Jeep, she was the guest of some religious community about which she knew nothing, except that they were very kind and offered lodging to strangers.

Her thoughts went to Jordan. She missed him now that she had grown accustomed to his cheerfulness in any situation. He, no doubt, was regaling Dr. Dan with one of his numerous and humorous adventures and planning how he would add this one to his repertoire. She closed her eyes and remembered the look in his eyes and the catch in his voice when he had given her the set of opals and diamonds. "Do you really not know *why* I gave them to you, Bergitta?" he had answered her query.

She hugged herself. She thought she knew, but he had stopped short of saying it. Could it be possible that the phony marriage was, after all, going to produce a real and lasting love between them? She knew the answer her heart was crying out for. She longed for the love of her husband. She longed to be held by him and cherished by him and to know they never need part again. Even so, would their love be as complete and beautiful as Mara's? She thought of her parents. Their marriage had a unity that came from their oneness in Christ. She had heard them say it many times. She wondered if Jordan knew anything about a life with God.

She had never heard him say.

She drifted to sleep to the sound of strange animal calls wafting on the soft, stirring breeze.

Jordan was waiting outside the community cafeteria at breakfast the next morning, looking as though this were his usual routine.

Bergitta made a face at him. "How can you be so disgustingly cheerful this early in the morning?"

He threw an arm around her. "Just one of the adorable attributes that you love me for," he grinned.

That was true, she admitted to herself, but not to him.

They sat down to a breakfast of meat patties served with a side of a thick white substance that had little taste. It was spread over a dark spongy bread, so Bergitta assumed it must be some sort of cheese.

"What are we going to do here all week?" Bergitta asked woefully and under her breath.

"I don't think *that* will be a worry," Jordan chuckled. "Dan spent most of the night planning all he wanted to talk about and catch up on. He's here on an interim assignment from Pennsylvania, and I'm sure he's abominably lonesome. But he seems to have a real heart for the work he's doing. There's an orphanage here and a Bible School that trains young men to go out and do their thing in the native tongue. Dan says it's a very efficient way of getting the gospel out, whatever that means."

Silently, Bergitta suspected Jordan would find out what it meant before the week was out. Dan would most likely discover the opportunity to tell him.

After breakfast, attending chapel services seemed to be generally expected. Not to go would have been an affront to their host, so Jordan and Bergitta slid into the last row of chairs under the outdoor shelter. Dan read from the Scriptures and the people sang from the heart.

There was a small disturbance near the door, and they turned to see Mara restraining Zhan-ta who was

150

doing his best to hobble toward Bergitta and Jordan. Jordan beckoned to let him come, and Zhan proudly twisted his small frame between them.

"Dr. Dan said I could be your guide while you are here," he beamed at them. Jordan nodded, and Bergitta noticed he did not seem to mind at all.

Classes convened after services, but Zhan offered to take them for a walk.

"Are you allowed to skip classes?" Jordan asked the child.

Zhan hung his head. "I don't take the classes."

"Why?" Jordan demanded sharply. "Only your leg is crippled. Your mind is fine."

The boy was silent.

Bergitta knelt beside the child. "We'd love for you to be our guide, Zhan. Thank you for asking."

Zhan led the way down the path, hobbling along on his stick. "I'm going to pick the bouquet for Mara's wedding, and she's going to let me read from the God Book at the marriage service," he said proudly.

"You and Mara are very close," Bergitta observed.

"She is my sister, my only living family," the child said. His face crimped up. "I will miss her when she leaves."

Tears came to Bergitta's eyes. "It's hard to give up someone you love Zhan, but perhaps you will visit her and her husband often."

He shook his head. "They will live far, far away."

The path they took led back to the Jeep, and Jordan removed the suitcases containing their clothing. He looked under the hood once again to make sure he had properly identified the broken part.

That evening, Dan, Jordan, and Bergitta stayed around the cafeteria table long after the others had gone. Jordan repeated the question to Dan that he had asked Zhan earlier.

"Why does he not attend classes with the other children?"

Dan sighed. "Why, indeed? We have one teacher to sixty children. Zhan's parents never sent him to school before they died, and when we got him barely six months ago, he was frightened to death of school. Also, since he has never had schooling, the teacher would have to give him special individual attention, and even if Zhan were willing, she wouldn't have the time."

"Is his reluctance due to his physical disfigurement?" Bergitta questioned.

"I'm afraid so. He has a mindset that he is 'different.' His parents were superstitious idol worshipers and told him the gods were displeased with him. He spends his life trying to please everyone, to win approval, but he is sadly lacking in the most important approval of all—self-approval," Dan said sadly.

Jordan shook his head slowly. "He's in for a hard time of it." He looked up. "Has a doctor seen and diagnosed the problem? Is his deformity caused by some crippling disease such as poliomyelitis, which I'm told is still seen in this part of the world?"

"As I said, he has been here only a few months, and we have no funds or government services to treat this kind of problem. As far as what caused the crippling, Mara says that when he was a toddler, he fell from a tree. She describes the leg as having been badly broken and twisted in two or three places. There was no doctor, and the leg simply healed in its broken configuration."

"Have you not examined him?" Jordan queried.

"I'm not a medical doctor," Dan explained. "My specialty is in social services and a good deal of seminary training."

"I see," Jordan said grimly.

A look of determination came on his face, and Bergitta knew he had made some sort of decision. She watched him curiously. The wheels were spinning in his head, and quite unexpectedly she found herself remembering other incidents in which Jordan had shown an inordinate amount of interest in the field of medicine. First, he had known exactly how to treat the motion sickness on the ship. Then there had been his handling of Dr. Halstrom. Now this. It made her wonder.

While the rest of the compound went about their daily routines, Jordan and Bergitta spent a lot of time with Zhan-ta. Jordan in particular took a special interest in gaining the child's confidence.

One day they were swimming by a waterfall that spilled into a shallow pool, and Jordan taught the boy how to slide down the slippery rocks into the cool water. Zhan laughed, a pitiful sound of pain mixed with pleasure. His little face was strangely contorted, pinched with pain, yet pierced with laughter.

"When does your leg hurt the most?" Jordan asked Zhan.

"It hurts the most all the time," the child told him.

"It would be good for you to do exercises in the water to strengthen your muscles. Try this one." Jordan demonstrated what he wanted Zhan to do and the child obligingly imitated him. He panted with pain, but kept on doggedly until Jordan told him to stop and showed him another exercise.

Bergitta watched them as she set out a picnic lunch the kitchen workers had provided. It suddenly dawned on her what Jordan was doing. He was expertly evaluating the damage to the leg as well as he could without the benefit of X-rays.

When they came out of the water, Jordan suggested Zhan take a rest on the air mattress they had brought in their safari gear.

"I'm going to press some places on your leg, Zhan, and I want you to tell me if it hurts."

Bergitta watched, fascinated, as she saw him make

mental notes during the informal examination of the deformed leg.

They ate the lunch of sandwiches and fruit, and over and over again she wanted to ask questions, but always Zhan was present.

"This is a lovely spot for a picnic," Jordan said appreciatively, looking around at the green meadow clearing and the rushing fall of water. Flowers grew at the edge and in clumps around the smooth, rounded rocks.

Zhan limped over to a patch of flowers as blue as the sky, using his sturdy stick for support to help him over the rocks.

"These I am going to pick for Mara's bridal bouquet," he explained, leaning over to pick the flowers.

"Careful, Zhan," Bergitta warned.

He slipped, and his stick went rolling across the rounded stone and splashed into the water. Jordan retrieved it while Bergitta helped Zhan back across the rocks.

They packed the leftovers from the picnic and started back.

Bergitta was determined to find some time alone with Jordan. Perhaps if she were tactful, he would talk about his findings with Zhan. Perhaps he would even open up and tell her about a part of his life that she now knew he had kept hidden in the past, for whatever reason.

When they returned, however, Dan was waiting for Jordan to join him in a game of chess, his chief pastime. He had been delighted to learn that Jordan played.

On her way to the dormitory, Bergitta passed several of the women coming from their Bible classes. She waved at the friendly round face of the woman who, according to camp gossip, was due to deliver her baby any day.

"Will they bring in a doctor?" Bergitta asked Mara when she returned to the room they shared.

"Nah!" Mara scoffed. "The women help each other

that way. Some of the older women have been to a lot of birthings and know just what to do."

Bergitta said nothing, amazed at their primitive way of life. She was so grateful for the advantages she would have when one day she gave birth.

Bergitta wasn't able to be alone with Jordan until late after dinner.

"How about a romantic walk in the moonlight, Mrs. Worthington?"

"Do you promise to protect me from the wild animals?" she bargained with him.

He facetiously growled and snarled, his eyes warning her that he was the one who would have to be kept at bay.

She laughed at his nonsense and thought what a good opportunity this was to ask him some of the questions that had been whirling around in her head all afternoon. But Jordan had other things in mind. As soon as they were out of sight of the camp, he pulled her into his arms.

"I've missed our private times together," he whispered, burying his face in her hair.

She lifted her lips to receive his kiss, and they clung together for several minutes before they continued the walk to the waterfall which was only a quarter of a mile down the path.

They sat on the flat rocks and she leaned against him.

"You look nice in khaki," she informed him. They had both worn their safari clothes since they had arrived at the camp.

"Ummmm," he murmured. "You look nice in anything—or out! Wanna go skinny dipping?" he teased.

"Don't hand me that old medical gambit about giving me an anatomy lesson!" she spoofed.

He looked at her strangely. "Where did that come from?"

"I thought you might tell me," she countered.

"There's nothing to tell," he said shortly. "Besides, who wants to waste time talking?"

He began a slow journey with his lips, up her slender neck, while he caressed her temples in a gentle circular motion with his thumbs. He stroked her face with his fingertips before claiming her mouth in a gentle sensuous kiss, teasing the corners of her sensitive lips beneath his. The moon had sped along its trek across the sky before he finally released her from his intoxicating kisses.

"I'd be tempted to keep you here all night if I thought they wouldn't send out a search party for us," he said in a voice wracked with passion.

"But they would," Bergitta pointed out, reluctantly rising to her feet.

"Come on. Let's have a good run," Jordan suggested, slapping her on the backside. She trailed him by several yards, and once or twice he stopped and waited for her, chiding her for having poor conditioning.

They said good night, and within half an hour Bergitta had showered and retired for the night.

Somewhere between midnight and dawn, she and Mara were awakened by a piercing scream.

"Zhan! Something has happened to Zhan! He has hurt his leg again." The girl began throwing on her clothes, fingers trembling and face perspiring with anxiety.

"Wait." Bergitta held her back. "It doesn't sound like him. Listen."

The screams were heard again in quick succession. "Oh, that poor woman," Mara moaned in sympathy. "She is having her baby."

The anguished screams were unsettling and left nothing to guess about the pain the woman was suffering. "Maybe she will have the baby quickly."

Bergitta and Mara consoled each other with white faces, for the screams made them realize that this was a

156

common fate shared by them.

The screams didn't diminish, and some time later the pounding of running feet could be heard against the hard-packed earth outside.

"I can't stand the suspense any longer," Mara declared. "I'm going to see what's wrong."

"I'll come with you," Bergitta offered quickly, "but we must not get in the way of those helping her."

They arrived just seconds after Jordan. Bergitta could see him inside the bedroom of the small, dimly illuminated cottage. He was leaning over the bed and appeared to be examining the woman's abdomen. His voice barked out orders to the women assisting, and they scurried to do his bidding. He began an arduous physical task, explaining to the woman in reassuring tones that he was going to have to turn the baby.

Bergitta dropped her face in her hands and discovered she was crying. "Oh God, help him to save her life," she prayed and was suddenly conscious that it was the first prayer she had prayed in years.

A small group had gathered. Bergitta suggested they all meet in the cafeteria and make a pot of coffee while they waited.

The cries of the woman weakened and finally stopped. No other sound could be heard in the dark night before the dawning.

Heads were propped in hands, some praying, some nodding off to sleep to awaken and pray again.

They looked up. The husband stood in the doorway. "My wife and I have a son. They are both doing well, thanks to Dr. Worthington."

Cheers went up, intermingled with praises to God. All of the group drifted home, except Bergitta. She stayed to pour Jordan's coffee, for she felt sure he would need it after the ordeal.

When he came, she ran to meet him, and they fell into each other's arms. He was shaking from exertion.

She stroked his back, as he leaned on her, finding her arms a haven.

She persuaded him to sit down while she brought his coffee which he downed in two gulps. He held the cup out for a refill. From bleary, red eyes he looked at her and said, "Bergitta, I have so much to tell you." His words were punctuated with pain and exhaustion.

"Yes, I know you do, but it can wait until tomorrow," she said.

Chapter Ten

By the time Bergitta awoke the next day, Jordan had been taken farther into the interior to treat an almost lethal wound to a native who had been gored by a wild boar. Dan had asked him to see as many of the dangerously ill as he could before leaving with the supply plane three days later.

Bergitta gulped back the tears. She had so been looking forward to being with him after last night's revelation. Now he was making a two-day trip on horseback. He would not return until the morning of Mara's wedding.

Mara sat on the little cot in the plain room she shared with Bergitta and bounced up and down excitedly.

"I have memorized my vows, but I am so afraid I will forget them," she squealed.

"You can practice on me," Bergitta smiled.

Mara wet her lips nervously as though this were the real thing. "Let's see. I say the ring vows right after Zhan reads from the God Book, as he calls it," she smiled.

Bergitta interrupted, "Zhan said he never learned to read. How will he be able to read from the Bible?"

"I taught him some of the psalms and passages from the gospels. He likes to hold the Book of God open and pretend that he is reading the Word," she smiled.

"Wouldn't it be wonderful if he could?" Bergitta said

dreamily, having grown very fond of Mara's winsome brother.

"I worry about him when I leave. There will be no one to look after his special needs."

They looked at each other helplessly. "Don't think about it now. Enjoy your wedding day, and the planning for it is an exciting part. Show me your wedding dress."

Mara smoothed the roughly woven, shapeless gray dress. "This is it. I have no other clothes."

Bergitta's mouth dropped open, but she quickly closed it again.

Mara's eyes twinkled. "Tell me about your wedding dress, and I will just imagine that I am wearing it in the ceremony."

Bergitta stood up and walked the distance of the room restlessly.

"Better yet, let's try to make you something." She pulled out from under the bed the small case that Jordan had brought from the Jeep. There was one sheer short nightie that she thought could be refashioned into a veil. For a dress, she considered the white sheet on the cot, but sheets were at a premium in the compound. Her eye caught the sleeping bag she had used the first night before a cot was brought in. It was the new one Jordan had bought her for the safari, and it was lined in white silk.

Her nimble fingers began to tear at the threads. "Is there a sewing machine around here, Mara?"

"An old one, but it works," she answered, wide-eyed, as she realized what her new friend was doing.

They worked on the dress the entire two days that Jordan was gone. At last Mara was trying it on for Bergitta to take the hem.

The young bride caressed the fabric roses that the designer had formed from the white silk. They framed the deep, low-curving décolletage that circled Mara's shoulders back and front. The lines of the dress nipped in at the waist and flowed to an ankle-length hemline. The veiling was of the sheer material of the nightgown.

"Wani will be so surprised," Mara said dreamily, anticipating the moment when her bridegroom's eyes would light up.

"Bergitta, I love you," she squealed and threw her arms around the slender woman. "You are like a sister." Her white teeth sparkled in a brilliant smile. "We are sisters in Christ, you know, and someday we shall go together to meet Christ our Bridegroom." The girl's voice had suddenly taken on a very serious quality. "Bergitta, I haven't asked you if you know Him. Will you wear the robe of the righteous when Jesus comes?" The loving words spilled over into the cavernous void in Bergitta's heart.

"I once knew Him, a long time ago when I was about your age," she answered the girl honestly.

"Promise me you won't be one of the foolish virgins who ran out of oil before the bridegroom arrived."

Tears sprang to Bergitta's eyes. "Perhaps that *is* what happened," the designer whispered. "You are a good friend, to care. Thank you, Mara."

Jordan returned the morning of the wedding. He sought Bergitta out immediately and invited her for a walk. It was the only way they could be alone.

As soon as they made the first bend in the path, he kissed her deeply, fully. "I missed you," he said with simple humility.

"And I missed you," she said, caressing his face in her hands.

"I'll be leaving with the supply plane at noon today, so I want to clear up what I know must be a big question mark in your mind."

"I know you are a doctor. I've suspected it ever since our visit with the Halstroms."

Thoughtfully, Jordan said, "My own story is not a great deal unlike Paul's. There are many forms of paralysis, Bergitta."

"What happened, Jordan?" she asked softly, slipping

161

her hand into his as they continued their stroll.

"I had finished my residency and was considering several offers among staff positions at hospitals and private practice, when another offer came in." He paused as though bracing himself against painful memories. He went on. "That offer came from the U. S. Surgeon General's office in Washington. They were recruiting volunteers for a research team to go into South America and study diseases peculiar to that habitat. The purpose was to know what inoculations to give military advisors going into that area to help those countries fight communistic infiltration of their governments."

"I don't have to guess which offer you took," Bergitta said dryly. "Your spirit of adventure rose to the call."

"That, mixed in with a little patriotism," Jordan said lightly. "I had not served any military time and thought this would be an opportunity to make my contribution."

They reached the waterfall and seated themselves on the flat boulder that jutted over the rushing stream. Bergitta plucked one of the blue flowers growing by the water's edge and twisted it thoughtfully in her hand. She looked at him questioningly.

"The rest of the story is ugly, and I wish it didn't have to be told," he went on. "I never talk about it to most people. But you are not 'most' people, Bergitta. You're special. If I am ever to talk about us, together, I must talk about this first."

"You make it sound grim."

"I'll tell you how grim it was," he frowned. "My cover as a research scientist was blown when an earthquake hit the village area where we were collecting data. The others were still in the laboratory conducting experiments, but I was in the village interviewing the people when destruction hit. I saw people injured and dying before my eyes. My natural response was to treat the emergencies even though we had been warned not to become involved with medical problems while on

162

assignment. Naturally, this caught the attention of the authorities who were communist puppets, and they began to investigate our work more closely. Although they could never prove that our project was any more than the innocuous textbook research we claimed it to be, the team was deported, and I was held for further questioning under house arrest. Naturally the State Department denied any knowledge of me other than as a member of the research project, and that saved my life.

"To make a point, however, they held me for six months while they were deciding on a disposition of the matter."

"Were you free to come and go?"

"Yes. There were never any formal charges." As an afterthought he added, "Except those self-flagellations for my own stupidity in reacting to the wounded instead of thinking about the consequences of discovery."

"I'm sure the people whose lives you saved were grateful you put life before country."

Jordan nodded. "Fortunately, no real damage was done. The information needed by our government had already safely crossed the border."

Sensing there was more, Bergitta said, "I have a feeling something very significant happened during those six months."

"True. I wasn't allowed to leave the village where I'd been working. The team had given me what was left of our supply of chemicals to purify the water. When that ran out, I was at the mercy of bacteria against which I had no natural immunity. I became dehydrated from dysentery, and no medical aid was available. Somehow, I survived, and I realized that my only hope was to drink their wine." Unexpectedly, he chuckled. "That stuff was poison. It was bound to kill anything that ailed me. It also kept depression at bay until I was finally released with orders never to visit their country again. I can tell you it wasn't a problem to agree to those terms!"

Bergitta laughed with him. "All's well that ends well. Right?"

"Wrong. My problem had just begun." He sighed heavily.

"Back in the States, I signed on to a staff position in a New York hospital and gradually began to realize that I had developed an alcohol dependency. I had never been a drinker to speak of, and it was difficult for me to admit that although the wine kept me from dying, its side effects were equally destructive. I couldn't practice medicine with good conscience any longer, not after I saw how my effectiveness as a physician was being destroyed by alcohol.

"I took a leave of absence and have spent the last year rehabilitating my life."

"Is that where Clare came in?"

"Yes. Most of what you read in the papers—I believe you described it as 'the world was my playpen'—was simply an attempt to escape the realities of my problem while I was going through treatment."

"I'm sorry, Jordan. I was pretty hard on you, when you actually deserved a commendation. It takes a strong person to deal so courageously with a problem. You even laid your career on the line."

"I don't know that I'd call it courage. I simply had no other choice."

"Did Clare know you were fighting this?"

Jordan nodded. "I'm afraid I used her as part of the escape."

"Well," she said stoutly, "you have certainly been a credit to your profession these last few days. A mother and child are living because of your skill. Are you ready to return to your profession?"

"I don't know," Jordan replied honestly. "After the difficult delivery the other night, if there had been a drink within ten miles, I would have found a way to get it. I thought I had the problem licked, but now I'm not so sure."

"Do you have to be sure, Jordan? This might be something you fight the rest of your life. Can't you just live one day at a time?"

He shook his head. "The risks in medicine are high enough without compounding them with a known problem."

He scooped up a handful of pebbles and began to toss them into the water one at a time. "Circumstances change us. I used to live to practice medicine. Now it seems even that is not enough. Adventure is not enough. What is 'enough,' Bergitta?"

How could she answer that, when she hadn't answered it for herself? She looked into his eyes honestly. "I don't know, Jordan. But I know this. You are a strong person. You don't look for easy answers. If you search in the right places, you'll find what is enough. If it means anything, I understand how you feel."

"I knew you would. Knowing you can count on someone to understand is half the measure of love."

"And what is the other half of the measure, Jordan?"

"For me, it's you and all that you are—the fact that you trusted me when I couldn't explain all about my past. Your beauty, your kind tender heart, your lively spirit, and your unselfishness—you are the most vital part of my life. I love you, Bergitta."

He stood and lifted her up. As he swept her into his arms, she gazed upward to receive the full impact of the stormy passion that burned in his eyes.

"And I love you, Jordan, with a completeness I would never have thought possible."

He caught her lips in a tender hungering kiss, which grew to burning intensity as his desire for her mounted.

She met his embrace with equal fervor, not sure whether the crashing in her ears was the gushing waterfall or the pounding of her heart. With a low moan he moved toward a sheltered grassy glade and would have pulled her down with him to the pleasant spot, but she glanced at her watch. "The wedding is due to start in an hour, and I promised to help Mara dress. We'll have to hurry!" she gasped.

Some of the women were putting the finishing touches on the open-air chapel. They had brought ferns and palms from the bog to decorate the sanctuary for the festive, holy occasion.

Bergitta ran to help Mara. "You look lovely," she smiled as she adjusted the large bow from which the veil fell. The dress was simple and girlish—perfect for innocent Mara.

"The only thing missing is your radiant bride's smile," Bergitta teased, puzzled by her friend's worried frown.

"No one can find Zhan," Mara explained. "He is supposed to read the God Book at the beginning of the ceremony."

"Don't worry. Zhan isn't about to miss the chance to read from his beloved God Book. He's been counting the days!"

The minutes ticked away and the sun climbed higher in the sky. To pass the time, the gathering in the sanctuary began to sing softly. It was the most beautiful music Bergitta had heard since she was a child. She realized the sound came from spirit-filled hearts.

Jordan joined her. "These people seem so full of joy even though they don't have very much that is of material consequence," he observed. "I've noticed it ever since I've been here. They seem at peace with the little they have."

With tears in her eyes, Bergitta turned to him and said meaningfully, "Yes, Jordan. They have found God to be enough."

Their eyes held as Jordan comprehended her meaning. "How lucky they are," he murmured.

"No, not lucky. They simply made a choice."

He seemed puzzled, but there was no time to pursue it as a frustrated bridegroom joined them.

"Mara refuses to start the ceremony without Zhan,"

the young man in the white suit said.

Bergitta started. "Is he still missing?"

"I saw him going toward the waterfall. He said he was going to pick Mara's bridal bouquet," Jordan said.

Just then they saw a small cloud of dust in the distance. Jordan smothered an expletive and broke into a run to help the little writhing, twisting figure hurtling across the ground, making a valiant effort to go the distance.

He swooped Zhan up in his arms. "What happened, Zhan?"

Through tears coursing down a mud-streaked face, Zhan wailed, "My stick busted. Now I'm all dirty and Mara will be ashamed for me to read the God Book at her wedding."

"No such thing," Jordan denied. "She's held up the wedding waiting for you." Zhan beamed at Jordan as he took the child off to get him cleaned up and ready for his part in the wedding.

To the strains of congregational humming, the bride floated down the aisle to meet her bridegroom.

The love that welded their hearts together was displayed on the countenances of the bride and groom for all to see. Bergitta thought of Mara's words: "Will you wear the white robe of the righteous when the Bridegroom comes?" Bergitta turned her heart to God in the same way she had as a child. "Father, forgive me for leaving your Son out of my life. I want to live for you in such a way that the threads of my life will weave the fabric of a robe of righteousness. Amen."

Dan performed a simple, but meaningful, ceremony. Zhan proudly "read" the words of the twenty-third Psalm, and the benediction was pronounced. Mara and her husband were united for life. *For life!* Bergitta stole a glance at Jordan. *Father, may Jordan come to know you, and may we spend our lives together forever*, she prayed silently. It was more a wish than a prayer, she decided forlornly. Jordan knew nothing of the things of

God, and she had certainly been no help these past weeks. Soon now, they would be returning to New York to go their separate ways. Deep within, she knew her heart would never be separated from him.

The groom was kissing the bride. Jordan and Bergitta's eyes flew to each other. It was an intimate moment, almost as though the declaration of commitment was theirs to have and to hold.

An engine hum broke the silence. As the crowd dispersed, Jordan turned quickly to Bergitta. "I'll be leaving in a few minutes. I talked with Dan earlier, and he agrees it would be a good thing to look into the possibilities for surgical correction on Zhan's leg while I'm gone. It may take a few days to make the arrangements. I have a friend in Paris who's a specialist. When I get back, I want us to take Zhan with us. Will you get him ready for the trip?"

Bergitta nodded. "Does Mara know?"

"Yes, Dan talked with her. She thinks it's a good thing."

Standing beside the plane, he cupped her face in his hands. "This is no place to propose to a wife," he grinned, "so I won't." He grew serious. "I can hardly wait for the next few days to be over. When we're together again, we have some decisions to make. Be thinking about it, okay?"

Even though the plane's engines were drowning out his words, she nodded, too full of love to answer. She watched the plane become a dot in the distance and felt that her heart had taken flight with it.

She wandered aimlessly about the compound, despondent on the one hand, yet already anticipating Jordan's return. She thrilled to remember his words. While nothing definite was decided, there was most definitely promise. He wanted her for his wife, and she wanted in every sense to be his wife!

For the first time she understood the analogy of the

church, the bride of Christ, anticipating the Bridegroom's return.

The week stretched before her, and Bergitta was sure it would be the longest of her life. She must think of something to make the time go faster. Now that Mara was gone, she was sure Zhan would be lonely, so she went to find him.

She found him nestled in the low crotch of a tree, hidden by the branches so no one could see his tears.

She played hide and seek behind the bush limbs until a slow grin crept out on Zhan's face.

"C'mon, Zhan," Bergitta coaxed him with a beguiling show of dimples, "let's go exploring the trails."

He went along willingly. Bergitta's exploration was more than a passing interest in what they might find along the jungle path. She had seen some of the women from the compound passing to and fro carrying baskets of cloth, and she was curious about the activity along the edge of the stream that flowed a hundred yards below the main buildings.

Women with their skirts draped and tucked around their knees were gathering a variety of plants. Farther down the creek bank dark liquid was boiling in great pots. Some of the women stoked the fire with wood while others punched a mass in the pot with long poles, stirring it.

Bergitta looked at Zhan questioningly.

"They are making dye from the plant leaves and weaving cloth from the tough stems. Then the cloth goes into the dye. Come, I show you."

They wandered through the small groups of willing workers who waved and smiled as they passed. Farther on they came upon a hut where crude handmade looms shuttled through the woof and warp of the threads. The resulting fabric was amazingly fine and smooth to the touch. One of the women allowed Bergitta to work the shuttle, much to her delight.

"Do you do this all the time?" she asked.

The dark-haired woman shook her head. "No, only when cloth is needed for clothes." Suddenly she grinned and whispered in Bergitta's ear, "Tomorrow we are weaving bed linens for Mara's wedding gift. You come and help if you like."

"I'd like very much!" Bergitta squeezed the woman's hand. She watched them work a while longer, and slowly an idea began to form. The fabric was gorgeous—just perfect for the line of children's wear she had been commissioned to design for the royal palace. Also, it would provide the trade relations with an underprivileged country as requested.

That night she waited in the cafeteria until all the others had gone. She stayed to have a last cup of coffee with Dan. She explained her idea to him, suggesting that if they had time to make extra fabric, the compound women could be well paid in order to improve their living conditions.

Dan was enthusiastic, and as they talked, the designer formed other uses for the fabric in her mind. Design House could no doubt use an endless supply of the finely woven fabric in the warm, earth-tone colors made from natural dyes.

"Of course, I'll have to perform tests for color-fastness and durability, but from what the women tell me, the cloth wears well."

The days passed, and though Bergitta was kept busy experimenting with combinations of the dyes to formulate new colors and working with the women to perfect the looming process, she still found herself with time on her hands to consider Jordan's "nonproposal." Most often that happened as she sat by the waterfall with her sketch pad, looking up from it to the far horizon where her dreams went to meet a speck that she hoped would appear in the sky any moment.

On these occasions she smiled reminiscently, floating back to a restaurant where they had held hands across the table in the candlelight, a chaste kiss before bedtime, fingers touching as she handed him a cup of coffee. She also remembered his pointed announcement that he refused to propose to her on the landing strip. He had to leave her hanging because the rest of his words were drowned out by the revving engines of the little two-seater plane.

No doubt he would save the proposal for some small, intimate French restaurant when they returned to Paris. There would be exotic food, floating candles among the lilies in a pool, and strolling musicians. She hugged herself in anticipation. Jordan had the sense of romance to make it a memorable occasion. The thought of Clare shadowed her daydreams just a little. She was troubled by the fact that he was unable to make a full disclosure about their relationship. *Or am I just being the proverbial jealous woman?* she wondered. She shrugged away her doubts.

As each day slipped by, her loneliness grew to chasmic proportions. She had no choice, she realized one day. Her heart had made the decision for her. He had become as necessary to her life as the air she breathed.

On the day he was to arrive, she dressed in eager anticipation. Her hands shook as she stepped into the freshly pressed safari outfit, woefully regretting that she had no wardrobe in which to look romantic and feminine for Jordan.

Zhan was restless with excitement, for he, too, would go with her and Jordan on the return journey in the Jeep, once the new part was installed.

They were never far from the landing strip. Bergitta felt as if she were fifteen again, waiting for her first date.

A dot appeared high in the sky and gradually dropped lower. She heard Dan's footsteps as he came to greet the plane. It was all Bergitta could do to restrain herself and Zhan from dashing onto the runway.

Bergitta began to wave as the small craft touched

down. Her hand slowed and her smile faded as the plane skidded past, and she saw it was occupied only by a pilot, and not even the regular one.

Her heart fell with a dull thud. On leaden feet she approached the pilot, her eyes wide with question marks.

"No return passengers?" Dan asked her unspoken question.

The pilot had an odd expression on his face and glanced in Bergitta's direction. "Perhaps I'd better see you in private, Dan."

Bergitta panicked. "I have to know now! Where is Jordan? Why didn't he come back with you?"

The pilot, Rick Lathem, introduced himself and looked at her sympathetically. "Mrs. Worthington, I can't answer your questions. We don't know where your husband is, nor the bush pilot and the plane that was carrying them. All we know is that the plane never arrived at its destination."

Bergitta looked at him in disbelief. "But surely if it was going down the pilot would have told the air traffic controllers. Wasn't there any radio contact?" She could feel her knees weakening under her.

The pilot shook his head in hopelessness. "They weren't flying in a monitored air corridor."

"Why not? That's against the law!" Bergitta snapped, her state of shock releasing anger.

Again, the pilot shook his head. "It's not against the law if you're flying line of sight."

Dan placed a hand on her arm and looked directly into her eyes. She could see the pain in his own eyes as he said, "Come to my office, Bergitta. There's something else you should know."

Sick with apprehension, she followed him across the air strip to the bare office in a barracks building. The pilot followed them.

After she was seated, Dan perched on the edge of his desk and told her, "The plane Jordan left on was carrying contraband. He was warned that it was a potentially dangerous mission, but he chose to go anyway. He said

172

he was no stranger to danger. He even seemed to anticipate the extra element of excitement."

"What kind of contraband? What kind of operation do you run here?" Bergitta cried, at the same time inwardly berating Jordan for his damnable sense of adventure. This time it could very well have cost him his life!

"Bibles!" the pilot hastily informed her. "The only way to get Bibles into the communist countries is to smuggle them across the border. On a refueling stop, a contact meets the plane, unloads the Bibles, then distributes them across the country by various means known only to the contact."

"Then the plane was in safe territory—right?"

Rick answered, "Unless they strayed over and violated neighboring air space. In that event the plane would have been brought down and searched."

Bergitta felt her body swaying and was grateful for the supportive arm Dan placed around her.

"It may help you to know that everything possible is being done to find them short of contacting the communist authorities. A search party is combing our side of the border. There's nothing we can do but wait and pray," the pilot said.

"Let's do that now, Bergitta," Dan suggested. She hardly heard the fervent prayer as grief and shock came together to rock her senses. So close she had come to having Jordan, just to have him snatched away!

It was a nightmare, Bergitta decided, when she awoke that night, tossing and turning on her bed. Reality seeped through and devastated her sleep. She was glad her parents had taught her to pray. She spent the night in a prayer vigil, petitioning for Jordan's and the pilot's safe return.

A prayer service was organized the next day. In so short a time Jordan had endeared himself to these people.

Dan called Bergitta into his office. "The plane is

ready to return. Don't you want to go home where you will be near family?"

She shook her head determinedly. "Jordan wanted me to bring Zhan with me as soon as he made arrangements at a hospital. I can't let either of them down. I'll wait here until Jordan returns, just as he expected me to do."

"Very well, then. Feel free to call on me any time. You're welcome here as long as you care to stay," Dan said kindly.

In her practical businesslike way, Bergitta used the time productively, though Jordan was never more than one thought away. Zhan was her constant companion, whether she was tackling some innovative sketch-pad creation or cutting swatches of fabric sample to take back with her.

Zhan kept up a steady stream of talk, mostly lining up all the things he had to tell Jordan when he came back for them.

Bergitta grew misty-eyed and remembered a Scripture that said, "Therefore be followers of God as dear children." Zhan seemed so free to follow God in faith and trust; she longed to have the same childlike trust that whatever the outcome, God's grace was sufficient to see her through.

"Mara used to read to me every day from the God Book." Zhan turned dark, earnest eyes to her.

"I would love to read the God Book to you, Zhan," Bergitta promised, and every day she did so.

It came alive. Its words of comfort bathed her wound with peace. God's love permeated her being and His promise was etched in her mind: "*And you will seek Me and find Me, when you search for Me with all your heart.*"

That was what God wanted most of all, she realized. He wanted *her* in a relationship with Him as her Father. At last she reached the place where she could surrender the circumstances to His keeping and praise Him for the circumstances to His keeping and praise Him for Who He was: omnipotent and omniscient eternal God!

"Bergitta! Bergitta! Come quick!" The child hobbled toward her breathlessly, his new stick thumping the ground. "Dr. Dan is looking for you!"

Bergitta scrambled up from the rock glades by the waterfall. "Did he say why?" she asked anxiously.

Zhan shook his head. "No. But the plane is here." Seeing her hopeful face, he said with childlike simplicity, "But Jordan isn't."

She tried to hurry, but her feet were leaden. It could be that word of his fate had come.

Dan and Rick stood as she entered. They were both smiling.

"We have good news for you, Bergitta. Your husband is safe."

Bergitta's collapse was every bit as traumatic as her response had been when she learned he was missing, so important had Jordan's safety been to her. She dropped her head on her knees and heaved heavy sobs. She felt Dan's big hand on one shoulder and a lighter one, Zhan's, on the other. He was grinning.

"You see? The God Book is true. We can trust God to keep His promises," the child said.

She grabbed him and hugged him, this child of faith. Of course God had acted according to His will, just as He had said He would to those who pray with believing faith.

She listened while Dan explained that the plane had developed engine trouble and had made a forced landing over the border. Officials had detained Jordan and the pilot for questioning, but since the contraband had already been dropped, there was no evidence to substantiate any claims of violating international law.

"Oh, praise God. Praise You, Father," Bergitta whispered over and over. "Where is Jordan now? When can I see him?"

Decisions were made expediently. Jordan was presently undergoing routine questioning and documentation of the incident at a U. S. military base in Germany. He had sent word he would meet her at the hotel in Paris where she was to bring Zhan. Arrangements had already been made to admit him to a hospital there.

She flew to get her bags and Zhan's. They had been packed and ready now for two weeks.

She said grateful goodbyes to Dan and those around. The plane lifted off, and the ground dropped away. She was only hours away from Jordan's arms.

Chapter Eleven

The familiar surroundings of the hotel were a welcome sight. In spite of the kindness of the new friends at the compound, it was good to get back to civilization.

Zhan was wide-eyed at the Parisian sights and was now standing somberly taking in the luxurious room with its French provincial white furniture. The carpets were raspberry and the drapes blue.

Bergitta settled Zhan in a comfortable chair with some picture books, then took a long relaxing bubble bath to refresh herself. In her daydreams she envisioned the time when Jordan would return and clasp her in his arms. A cablegram had been waiting at the hotel desk telling her his time of arrival—two o'clock tomorrow afternoon! Bergitta hugged herself.

After Zhan was tucked in bed that night, she sat down and thumbed through a stack of fashion magazines featuring the Design House showings. She had a few poignant moments as she looked at the bridegroom who was a stranger, but who looked so adoringly at her in the magazine pages. Today, she and Jordan were no longer strangers. They were deeply in love as she had never known love could be. The very thrill of seeing his image on the page was almost too much to bear.

Thank God the nightmare of his disappearance was over. She closed her eyes and relived those moments when she had first learned of his safety. As if that were not enough, she cherished the message Jordan had sent by the pilot who was to fly her back to Paris. He had wanted her to know that he had something extra special to share with her, something that would change their lives. Bergitta didn't have to guess what that was. Jordan wanted a lasting marriage with her. She pictured the sweet moment when he would make her his wife in every sense.

She flipped the pages and continued to read the reports. There was a consensus of editorial opinion that Design House had produced the fashion event of the season. Her own classical signature was sprawled across the pages and pages of her original designs. Bergitta sighed with ecstasy, knowing it was not possible to be happier than she was at this moment.

Having finished her concentrated evaluation of the layouts, she was just about to lay the magazine down when it fell open to a page which featured the familiar face of Clare L'aimant. Startled, she gasped, barely muffling the sob that tore from her lips. The model was pregnant! A photographer had made the shot on a secluded beach and had scooped the news to the magazine.

Bergitta gnawed at her clenched fists in anguish, almost faint from the shock. The child could only be Jordan's! She laughed mirthlessly. No wonder the prima donna model had been unable to appear for her wedding! No wonder Jordan had regularly sent her money and happily received her phone calls!

She thrust her head into her hands and leaned forward against her knees, weeping. Jordan had played her for a fool after all, never giving up trying to use her until the bitter end. Now she understood why he said he had something special to tell her that would change their lives. He undoubtedly was going to tell her that he and Clare were going to have a child and that now that the marriage charade was over, he was going back to her!

Stormily, she hurled herself across the room and dragged her suitcase from the closet.

The sleeping Zhan sighed and moved in his sleep.

The child! She couldn't abandon him. Bergitta groaned. She would have to stay until he was safely in Jordan's custody. Then she would leave for New York immediately to start annulment proceedings before Jordan had the chance to humiliate her again.

She changed into her blue silk nightgown and woodenly went about her nightly routine of applying night cream and brushing her beautiful length of hair to a shine. She was numbed by her discovery. She supposed anger would come later, but right now she could only swallow hard. Her love for Jordan was still real and settled like a hard knot in the pit of her stomach.

In bed, she fanned the sheets restlessly, trying several times to make excuses for Jordan, but she gave it up. Integrity demanded that she no longer play games about their relationship.

She slept at last, as the first ray of day brought the city into dawn's shadow.

"Bergitta! Bergitta! Wake up!" Zhan tugged at the bed covers. "You were going to take me to the Eiffel Tower today, remember?"

The exhausted young designer struggled up through waves of unconsciousness before finally focusing on the child's face. She groaned and rolled over, but the eager Zhan was insistent.

Bergitta went through the motions of brushing her teeth and applying her makeup while thoughts whirled in her pounding head. Jordan was going to be a father! What man wouldn't consider that a life-changing experience? She smiled bitterly.

Like unbidden dreams thoughts filtered through from the past several weeks. Jordan had explained his reason for sending Clare money was that she was out of work. Well, at least he was honest! A high-fashion model who

179

was more than halfway through her pregnancy would find few jobs.

She burst into fresh tears, ruining her makeup. "Oh, God!" she moaned. "Where were you? Why did you let this happen? I asked for guidance!" She called herself up short. She would not blame or question God. Jordan had won her heart, but he would not cause her to lose her soul.

Somehow, she got through the day with Zhan hobbling along beside her to distract her as they went on the sightseeing tour. Through it all there was a dull ache in her heart, and Bergitta knew it was the broken love that lay there in a million pieces. How could she have been so wrong in trusting him?

The hours were interminable. No longer was there the eager anticipation to see Jordan, but instead a dread at what she knew she must confront. She was going to enjoy turning the tables on him. For once, he would know what it was like to be the one injured. Deep inside her, Bergitta knew the lashing out was only a massage to her aching ego. It hurt miserably for Jordan to have betrayed her. It was a hurt from which she knew she would never recover.

After lunch, while Zhan took his nap, Bergitta made reservations with an airline for a flight to New York that evening. Then she packed her bags.

She dressed carefully, determined that Jordan would see her at her best. She fitted the original silk design against her sensuous curves. It was so beguiling it would even upstage the looks of the infamous Clare! The soft sea-green color against her creamy skin and dark umber hair made her look like the sylph of summer.

She knew that Jordan would have expected them to meet him at the airport. She watched the clock hands move to the two o'clock position. So much for his first disappointment.

The phone rang. Because she was in the bathroom

applying fresh makeup, Zhan answered.

"It's Jordan," the child caroled in glee. "He wants to speak to you!"

"Tell him I cannot come to the phone now and that I will see him when he gets to the hotel."

Moments later a somber Zhan appeared in the doorway. "He was unhappy that you did not speak with him."

Not half as unhappy as he is going to be when I get through with him, Bergitta seethed to herself, a malicious gleam in her eye.

Bergitta and Zhan were waiting out front when Jordan's cab arrived. Pushing Zhan ahead of her into the middle of the seat, she climbed into the cab. Answering Jordan's surprised look, she said, "We barely have time to make a three-o'clock appointment at the hospital for Zhan."

Jordan looked surprised and puzzled at the same time. He would have reached for her, but her cryptic attitude made it apparent that she was in no mood for sweet embraces.

"The appointment was for later this afternoon," Jordan pointed out.

"I found it necessary to change it. I have to fly back to New York this evening."

"Is something wrong at the office?" he asked with quick concern.

"Only that I have been away from my desk much too long," she shot back.

He settled back in silence as Zhan looked from one to the other.

At the hospital Bergitta kissed Zhan goodbye and promised to send him pretty cards often, then preceded Jordan from the room.

She was all the way down the hallway when Jordan caught up with her and wheeled her around by the shoulder. "What's going on, Bergitta? Can't you at least be civil? After all I've been through, this is hardly the

181

kind of welcome I expected."

"I'm glad you were not harmed, Jordan," she said coolly. "Now if you will excuse me, I have a plane to catch."

She shrugged his hand away from her shoulder and started walking. Without missing a beat, he strode along beside her. "If you think you're going to walk out of my life this easily—"

"It isn't easy," she interrupted him.

"Then what is it?" he demanded. His eyes burned through her, and to her chagrin, her tears started falling.

She pressed the elevator button. They maintained silence since there were several other occupants, but once out on the street, Jordan resumed his inquisition while Bergitta hailed a cab.

Undaunted, he slid into the seat beside her.

"You *are* going to talk to me before you leave," he rasped.

Her only retort was silence. She could hardly stand to look at his countenance which was a mixture of hurt, anger, and disappointment. She steeled herself against a temptation to give in to her feelings and throw her arms around him.

In the hotel room his eyes followed her as she set about gathering her things. He released a long sigh.

"This isn't at all what I expected, Bergitta," he said quietly.

She glared at him stonily. "Did you expect a hero's welcome, Jordan?" she asked with feigned sweetness. "A hero is more than a daring adventurer who triumphs over danger. A hero has honorable character."

Anger burned white-hot in his face. His body was as taut as a stretched spring. "I don't know what you're talking about, Bergitta."

"Oh, don't you? Did you really think I wouldn't find out?" She walked over to the chair and handed him a copy of the fashion magazine opened to Clare's photograph.

182

"I might offer you congratulations on becoming a father," she said with a quiver.

He glanced at the photograph without emotion. "And I might accept them if congratulations were in order. I can think of no joy greater than being a father. However, I'm afraid it is Chris who deserves the congratulations."

"Chris?" Bergitta blanched. "*Chris*—our photographer?"

"Chris, Clare's photographer—and her lover!"

She sank into the nearest chair.

"I wish you could have trusted me until you knew the facts," he said disappointedly, his eyes censuring her with their pain and disillusionment. "However, I suppose I do owe you an explanation. I'll be brief, since you wish to return to New York so speedily." His tone cut her like a knife.

He shoved his hands into the pockets of his tweed trousers and walked to the wide windows that looked out on the cloud-shrouded city. Rain fell in silver strips from the edge of the hotel's balcony, seeming to enclose them away from the rest of the world.

"Clare was on assignment in the Caribbean for four months before the wedding was to take place. I didn't see her the entire time. Chris was the photographer on the project, and in no time at all, he and Clare were involved. I didn't know this until just before the wedding when some friends who live in the islands told me that Clare and Chris were a name about town.

"At first, I assumed she was just being her fickle self, and I knew by then that she had only been a conquest for me."

He paused. The steady drum of the rain synchronized with the steady beat of his voice as he slowed to a less tempestuous pace.

"The night before our marriage, she called my father's house and asked to borrow money for an abortion. You see, Clare and I have been friends from

183

childhood. This isn't the first time I've helped her out of a financial jam while she was out of work. Instead of loaning her the money for an abortion, I offered to see her over the next several months if she would let the baby come to full term." His eyes glowered as he said, "You understand that was for the baby's sake, not Clare's. I am not one of these doctors who take human life lightly."

Bergitta gasped at his announcement. "Why hadn't she gotten an abortion early on?"

"There were physical complications threatening to her own life."

He sighed. "I thought that was the end of it, but a month later when she called, it was to say that Chris had found out, thought the child was mine, and was threatening to blackmail both of us. When he showed up in front of the bank in Switzerland, that was exactly why he was there—to extort money from me. That's where I drew the line and told Clare she would have to handle her own problems. In answer to her concern that Chris was going to expose the Design House wedding as a hoax, I told her as far as I was concerned, the marriage was anything but a hoax because I was deeply in love with my wife and always expected to be." He looked at her through suffering eyes. "That was the absolute truth, Bergitta, and it still is."

She gulped and whispered weakly, "Who took the picture? Was it Chris? Is he going to try to embarrass Clare and Design House anyway?"

"No. When Chris rejoined the ship a day late and I called him aside, I knew his rebellion against ship's rules was because he had a burr under his saddle. After all, I had thwarted his blackmail plans. To defuse any further plans he might have to set off a stick of dynamite, I told him the truth, that he was the father of Clare's child. He wrestled with that for a while, but finally he accepted it and insisted on knowing where Clare was. I got her permission, and the last I heard, he

184

was on the way there. This photograph is the work of a proud father, I suspect."

Bergitta swallowed hard and blinked back the tears. "You did what was right, of course. I just wish you could have trusted me enough to tell me sooner."

"There was no reason to tell you in the beginning. We were only playing a role—remember?" he said firmly. "When we got serious about each other, you were already having a difficult time accepting that Clare and I were through, and I didn't know just how far your fragile belief in me would hold. Besides, I'm still a doctor, and it's ingrained in me that a patient's confidence is privileged information."

When Jordan turned to face her, she was shocked by the grief in his face. She had been so wrong that she wanted to apologize, but an apology would only sound like an excuse. Helplessly, she stood motionless, hoping for some direction as to what to do next.

She waited, hoping for him to move toward her in the eons of silence that followed. He didn't, nor did he relax his rigid stance to allow her to approach him. Bergitta tried to speak, but there were no words.

He moved restlessly. "This isn't at all how I envisioned our meeting," he told Bergitta sadly. "I had something to share with you—something special that I thought you would understand."

She put out her hand to him. "Please, Jordan. I would like to hear," she pleaded softly. "I know you went through a very difficult situation, and I selfishly allowed my own concerns to overshadow what must have been a terrible ordeal."

Surprisingly, he replied, "To the contrary. It was the best thing that has ever happened to me. It was the beginning of the most exciting adventure of my life."

She looked at him curiously. His face had a glow. He continued to speak.

"Once we landed and were picked up by the border guards, I thought it was all over, but I noticed the pilot seemed unperturbed. Not only did he not panic; he was in complete control of the situation, so much so that the guards began to be curious about what was in the books we were smuggling. He offered to show them. They brought one of the contraband Bibles to him, and he showed them Scriptures that promised them freedom. Believe me, that caught their attention. The pilot read to them from the Gospel of John. There was a holy Presence that held them spellbound. Even I could sense it. He invited each of them to pray with him, that they might receive Christ, who pardons sin and gives freedom of the heart."

His next words poised over the silence. "I was caught up in the moment and found myself making a decision, too." A mist came into his eyes. "Bergitta, I accepted Christ as my Savior."

Bergitta crossed the room to him and offered him her hands. He took them in both of his.

"Jordan, I'm so glad for you—for both of us—because you see, I made a recommitment of my own life. It makes a difference, doesn't it?" she smiled.

"Yes, it does," he answered solemnly. "The long search for myself is over." He tucked her arm in his and walked her to the sofa. "I have a feeling that this new life is the greatest adventure yet," he grinned down at her. "Do you mind?"

"Not at all," she shook her head.

The rain was only a drizzle now. Late afternoon had darkened the room. "What about the future, Jordan?" She held her breath, waiting, hoping for the crucial answer.

"I will return to medicine," he said promptly. "I know I now have a source of strength that will be sufficient."

"But what about us, Jordan?" Bergitta's softly spoken question held a plaintive longing.

Jordan looked at her uncertainly. "I don't know, Bergitta. All I could think of during those nights away was that I had your trust, and that was all that mattered to me. Love isn't worth much without it. But now it seems your trust was more fragile than I thought. I'm not sure you have the trust it takes to build a marriage on."

"That's hard, Jordan!" Bergitta cried.

"Marriage is hard," he replied in steely tones.

Moving restlessly to the window again, he folded his arms across his chest and stood looking at her. He was so solid, so dependable, that she wanted to rush to him and force him to take her in his arms.

Instead, she stood still as deadly words dropped heavily from his lips. "For the present, I think it would be best if we proceed with the annulment. Perhaps after a fresh start...who knows?" he said musingly.

Starting for the door he admonished, "You don't have much time to make your plane. I'll go and hold a cab while you call for a bell captain to get your bags."

She stood rooted to the spot and remained there as his hand was on the doorknob. He raised his eyebrows quizzically.

"I'm not going anywhere, Jordan," she said, having made a sudden decision. She snared his gaze with hers and said with deliberation. "It's true that trust is important to a marriage, but so is forgiveness."

The brilliant eyes narrowed under the hooded brows. "What are you saying, Bergitta?"

Never wavering, she replied, "I've disappointed you. I'm asking your forgiveness. I love you so much I can't imagine life apart from you. Isn't forgiveness just as vital to love as trust?"

She opened her arms to him and in a moment they were together. His kiss was tender as he held her close, stroking her silken hair.

"I was afraid I had lost you, Jordan. I was afraid you had gone and taken my heart with you."

"Oh but Bergitta. You had my heart. I never could have given it to another."

187

He lifted her in his arms and carried her to the wide bed. Her arms crept around his neck as she cuddled against him.

"I love you, Mrs. Jordan Wright Worthington III," he muttered huskily. His lips covered hers and Bergitta knew that love's design was complete.

Forever Romances are inspirational romances designed to bring you a joyful, heart-lifting reading experience. If you would like more information about joining our Forever Romance book series, please write to us:

Guideposts Customer Service
39 Seminary Hill Road
Carmel, NY 10512

Forever Romances are chosen by the same staff that prepares *Guideposts*, a monthly magazine filled with true stories of people's adventures in faith. *Guideposts* is not sold on the newsstand. It's available by subscription only. And subscribing is easy. Write to the address above and you can begin reading *Guideposts* soon. When you subscribe, each month you can count on receiving exciting new evidence of God's Presence, His Guidance and His limitless love for all of us.